TROUBLE IN PARADISE

JACKI KELLY

TROUBLE FROM PARADISE

Jacki Kelly

Copyright 2019 by Kelly, Jacki

ISBN: 978-1-9422202-27-1

First Edition Electronic April 2018

Published by Yobachi Publishing, LLC

❀ Created with Vellum

This book is dedicated to my family, who always understands when I close the office door and ignore their questions. You guys support me in the most unbelievable ways, and I thank you.

CHAPTER 1

Lawrence Cistos eased into the sturdy chair behind his desk. His ample backside hung over the sides, but no one dared comment on his girth or attitude. Both needed an adjustment, but in his line of work, these characteristics were beneficial. When his size didn't intimidate his opponent, his attitude took care of the job.

He looked across the mahogany desk at the two men sitting in front of him. They were adequate for his purposes. Between the two of them, there were enough muscles to supply a small army.

Lawrence cleared his throat. "This meeting will be short. You're aware of my expectations. You've been briefed. Kais Bisset has assured me the painting arrived on Sebastian Island, and the tracking device I had installed confirmed the same thing…until it went offline. The last verified location is a warehouse unit guarded by a company owned by some security expert named Xander Fitzgerald. Fitzgerald's good, but you guys are supposed to be better. Based on my last conversation with Kais, he's backing out of the deal because either he thinks he can get more for the painting or he found out why it's so important to me. He obviously doesn't know me or my reputation. I want that corrected." The anger in his gut filled his voice.

"Give us the signal. We've got several men ready and waiting."

"This meeting is the damn signal. Did you think you were here for a fucking tea party?" He studied the men. He didn't know either of their names and had never met them before. If things went according to plan, he'd never see them again.

"Find my painting. I want the print buried in the frame. Up to now, I've been a patient man, but I have my limits." Lawrence pounded the desk. "Kais is stupid and greedy and well out of his league if he thinks he can negotiate against me. We had a deal. He's made an unfortunate error." Spit landed on the wooden desk.

Both men pushed to the edge of their chairs. Their unified movements and head nodding had to be something they practiced.

Lawrence slid the fat, white envelope across the desk. "Here's the retainer. You'll get the balance when I get my painting and print. Make sure the print is in mint condition."

The thug seated closest to the desk reached for the envelope, extracted the cash, and threaded the bills through his fingers. Afterward, he shoved the package into the breast pocket of his suit jacket. "Are there any limitations on how far we can go?"

Lawrence stood and pointed his finger at the one doing the talking. "I want my property. I don't care about Kais Bisset or anyone else. I've shelled out good money. If someone gets in the way, handle it."

CHAPTER 2

Olivia pulled the long sheath up her slender legs and wiggled the tight material over her hips. After slipping her arms through the spaghetti straps, she examined herself in the mirror. "Tell me again about the party," she yelled to Xander. He stood in the large closet trying to determine which tie to wear with his dark blue suit.

"Eliza and Kais are clients. They're into rare art. Not the kind found in the tourist shops here on the island, but the kind of pieces that make their way into MoMA in New York or the National Gallery in Washington. The sort of stuff regular folks like us can't afford."

"I wouldn't call you regular folks and they certainly aren't average either. They're wealthy."

"They aren't just wealthy. They invented the word for the people on the island. The folks on Sebastian kinda look at them like royalty – not the Windsor Palace type, but a smaller, lesser-known kingdom somewhere."

"Why are they offering their place for our wedding? I know they're good friends of yours, but still that's over-the-top." She pressed her back against the doorjamb and studied Xander. They hadn't set a date yet for their wedding and it wasn't because Xander hadn't tried. If he pinned her down and forced her to talk about why she was hesitant, she'd probably shrug her shoulders like a child who had forgotten to do her homework. She had no real reason. Marriage was permanent. Her parents had been married for over thirty years and the way her father still kissed her mother every morning was magic. But people their age didn't have marriages like that anymore. And if she couldn't imagine a life like that, there was no way she was going to go running into marriage and promise forever when she wasn't sure it existed. Yes, she was afraid. She and Xander had a good thing, and they were happy. There was no use messing it up by getting married because someone else like her parents, his parents, and her friends, expected it.

"Kais is a bit of a show-off. He's new money rich and loves to flaunt his wealth. Hosting our wedding would give him an opportunity to brag." Xander adjusted the blue and white tie around his collar. "How do I look?" His lips curled into a glorious smile. The room seemed to swirl around them. Moments like this… this state of happiness that she wasn't ready to start poking at with the reality of her doubt, made her feel singled out and special.

Her heart swelled. She would always feel this intense love for him, but would he be able to return her affection with the same consistency? "You look wonderful as always." She closed the gap between them and wrapped her arms around his trim waist. "They're Luc's parents and you adore your godchild, but they're odd. Their relationship seems fake. I've never seen them kiss or hold hands or even touch each other. I'm not sure I'd want someone to use one of the most important days of our lives as an opportunity to make a statement. Our love for each other is the statement."

"Tonight, is just a dinner party. We'll look around, pretend we're interested and tell them we'll get back with an answer. Besides, how can we commit to anyone, when you won't even confirm a date?" He towered over her and lifted her chin with his thumb. The way he locked eyes with her left her breathless.

She pressed up on her toes and covered his mouth with hers. The kiss was too passionate for two people dressed and on their way out the door, but she couldn't pass up the opportunity.

"You'll do almost anything to avoid picking a date, won't you?" His voice was light and casual, but his eyes weren't smiling.

Picking a date wasn't the hard part. It was everything that could happen afterwards. Would marriage mean giving up her independence, her choice? Would it mean living with Xander's chaotic schedule, dangerous assignments, and fitting her life around his? A year of stalking by Ajay, had changed her. Xander was nothing like Ajay, but that didn't lessen her fear that marriage would have an adverse effect on them both.

"I'm taking my time. We don't need to rush." She rubbed his arm. "We're going to marry only once. I want to make sure we do it right. Besides, your business is so nonconventional, you might have a case that requires months. Are you going to stop taking cases long enough for us to pick a date?"

"You're stalling." He held her gaze. "I'd stop tomorrow if I thought that was holding up the decision."

"You even promised to take me to the shooting range so I'd get better, and you haven't done that yet either. Suppose another kook decides to bust into our home and you're not here? I need to feel comfortable protecting myself."

"Bae, we had that conversation a long time ago. Stuff like

that doesn't happen on Sebastian Island. You're not in New York. Besides, I like you as a girly-girl."

"Didn't I show you how tough I can be when it came to Ajay? I left that man in tears."

He pressed his hip into hers. "Baby, we'll get to it. I promise. There's no rush. Right now, nothing is going on in the business that will put anyone in jeopardy." He paused. "You better be glad I'm in love with you, girl. I don't usually wait this long for anyone." He pinched her butt.

"And you better be glad I'm the levelheaded person. When that shaman tried to convince us that our ancestors wanted us to fork over five thousand dollars to protect our love, I swear you were reaching for your wallet."

"I was not." He smirked. "Now, let's get outta here. The party starts in ten minutes, and Eliza hates when her guests arrive late."

"Well, she's going to be miffed tonight, because we won't be there at eight." Olivia stood in front of the jewelry drawer and selected a pair of dangling earrings. Something about Eliza made her uncomfortable. Her familiarity with Xander was questionable. "How do you know so much about Eliza?"

He slipped his arm around her waist and started her toward the door. "You look perfect. Let's go."

"Yeah, that's a question we'll come back to."

CHAPTER 3

In the car, Xander caught a glimpse of Olivia's profile as he made the turn onto the Bissets' grand lane leading to their mansion. They hadn't talked during the few minutes it took to drive over. Olivia was probably chewing on the fact that he wouldn't discuss Eliza and Kais. It wasn't just because they were clients. There was no need to pull out his past and spread it out before Olivia for her approval or disapproval. She had nothing to worry about. Eliza was a long time ago, before she married Kais and long before he met Olivia. He and Eliza both knew it was only a sexual fling. Eliza hadn't wanted anything other than a few dates and nights of hot sex. He had wanted someone to help him forget Hope, and Eliza filled that role.

Olivia was stalling, and every day she waited before setting the date made him sweat a little bit more. Something had spooked her. A few months ago, dresses and colors and wedding cakes and menus were the only things she wanted to talk about. Now, every time he brought up the subject, she jumped to another topic. If she didn't come up with a date they both could agree on, he was going to go ballistic. Somewhere in history, it was decided that women picked the date, did all the planning, and were the only ones to have prenuptial excitement. Why was the woman he wanted to marry so different?

She'd even dashed his biggest hope that she'd come down the aisle in a gown that made her look like a princess. He was willing to accept an African princess, but now she seemed to be leaning toward a two-piece number that exposed her belly and hugged her ass. As long as she came down the aisle, she could be naked.

Xander slowed the car and pointed through the passenger side window. "That's the place. Imagine an evening reception with the house lit up like that." He liked the idea and could only hope it didn't make her regurgitate.

She followed the direction of his finger. The Bisset mansion glowed like a diamond sitting on the top of the hill. "It looks great." Her tone was as noncommittal as everything else concerning their wedding.

"You're faking enthusiasm. I know you well enough to know the difference," he said.

"I want to see the inside first."

"Okay. I won't ask you again until the end of the evening. I'm not trying to pressure you. I just want to marry you."

He drove up the steep driveway and into the line of cars waiting for the valet. He threw the keys to a guy that couldn't be old enough to have graduated from elementary school.

The double-wide glass doors were opened for them as they approached. From the entry, the opulence of the house was evident. The crystal chandelier with teardrop crystals sparkled like rays of sunshine. A butler stood just right of the door to take Olivia's wrap and another one offered them drinks.

"Does all this come with the wedding?"

"If you want." He bit back the excitement that she might be impressed.

Guiding her by the elbow, Xander led Olivia through the adjoining room, walking slow enough for the elegance to stun her into getting the wedding process moving.

Kais spotted him from across the room and headed toward them. "I've been waiting for you to arrive. Hello, Olivia, so good to see you again." He smacked Xander on the back and air-kissed Olivia's cheek.

"Will I get a chance to see my godson? He hasn't gone to bed yet has he?" Xander asked.

"Luc is getting ready for bed. The nanny will bring him downstairs shortly."

"Maybe he can come to the house next week. We're due for an adventure."

"Do you have a moment? I need to speak to you in private." Kais ' eyes shifted around the room.

"We just got here, Kais. And I hadn't planned to talk business tonight. I'm out with my fiancé." He tightened his hold on Olivia. Her hand slipped to his ass, and he couldn't help but smile.

"Leave him alone, Kais. You can talk later." Eliza came to stand beside her husband. "It's so good you two could make it. I'd love to host your wedding here." Eliza beamed, pointing out the elegance of the room.

"I really need to talk with Xander for just a moment. I promise I won't hold him long. Olivia, you don't mind, do you?"

"No, it's okay." Olivia kissed Xander's cheek. "Go ahead, honey. It will give me some time to talk with Eliza about our plans for the wedding."

"Do we have plans?" Xander lifted his eyebrow.

"I have ideas," Olivia said.

Kais grabbed him by the arm and tugged him across the

room. "I'll only be a few moments." He called to Olivia before Kais pulled harder.

"What the hell is wrong with you, Kais?" Xander tried to sound calm, but he couldn't hold back his irritation. "I am not on the clock twenty-four hours a day. If I'd known you wanted to discuss business, I wouldn't have come."

"I'm in trouble. A lot of trouble, Xander, and I need your help."

Xander squared his shoulders. "It can't wait until tomorrow?"

"No. I haven't shared this with Eliza yet, but he's threatening to kill me. And I believe he's serious. I think this goon is capable of anything."

"Who the hell are we talking about?"

"I don't know his name. He wanted all transactions between us to be anonymous." Kais' eyes darted around the room.

"Kais, you're an established businessman. Why were you doing business with a faceless person?"

"Look, Xander. I do business with all kinds of people. Some like to keep their identity secret for good reasons. It doesn't mean they're shady characters." Kais' voice had a definite edge.

"Okay, calm down." Xander pointed to the chairs. "Let's sit and you tell me what's going on. So, you're being threatened. And you have no idea who these threats are coming from?"

"No." Kais stared down at his hands.

"Let me come at this another way. What does your no-name client want?" Xander tugged at the collar of his shirt. Either the room was getting warmer or he was.

"The Renoir is missing from the warehouse. That painting is worth five million. Jeffrey called me a few days ago and said it was missing."

"Who the fuck is Jeffrey?" Xander crossed his foot over his knee to observe Kais. He was sweating too much for a man telling the truth.

"He's one of my men. I sent him to the warehouse to retrieve the painting. I had a buyer for it, and it's gone." Kais jumped up from the chair and wiped his forehead on the sleeve of his silk jacket. "I'm not sure why the buyer has gotten so angry. It wasn't authenticated, and I offered to return his money. Now it's gone, and he says if I don't give him his painting, he's going to kill me."

"The painting was in the warehouse we've been guarding for you? That little storage unit?" Xander pushed out of the chair and walked up behind Kais. "Why don't I believe you, Kais? My gut tells me you're lying about something."

"Just find out who's threatening me. That's all I'm asking you to do."

"How could someone break in and we not know? We have someone there twenty-four hours a day. Why didn't you contact me when you heard about this?" Xander measured his words. Losing his temper with a client was never a good idea.

"It happened yesterday. I didn't think it was anything to worry about until I got a call before my guests started arriving this evening."

Xander widened his stance. "Let me get this straight... You've got a client willing to pay five million for a painting that you know isn't authentic, and the painting has gone missing. Even though it's under watch by two men." He rubbed his chin. "You were going to sell the painting to someone else and you decided to tell me about all of this when your life was threatened. Does that sum up your story?"

Kais spun on him. "I know it doesn't sound good, but can you help me? I'll pay you."

"You'll pay me?" Xander didn't hide his disdain. "How about you just be honest with me."

"I'm telling you the truth." Kais looked down at his shiny patent leather shoes.

"Have you been to the warehouse to check for yourself?"

"No. No one knows I own that space, and I want to keep it that way."

"Well, someone knew you owned it if your painting is gone." Xander walked to the windows overlooking the garden. It was too dark outside to make out the lush flowers and the tropical plants. Hopefully, Olivia was enjoying the party enough to set a wedding date. "What does Jeffrey have to say? Have you talked to him?"

"I can't reach Jeffrey. He's not picking up."

Xander fished his phone from his pocket and pointed it at Kais. "I wasn't supposed to be working tonight. I don't like breaking promises to my fiancé." He scrolled through his contact list until he found his assistant's number.

"Yeah. I thought you weren't working tonight. Why are you calling me?" Omar sounded sleepy.

"Yeah, well. Look, who has the Bisset warehouse shift tonight?"

"Do you expect me to know the answer off the top of my head?" Omar said.

"Check it. Call him and get a full report. Then call me right back. I want to know if everything down there is okay."

"Got it. Anything else?"

"No. Not until you report back." He disconnected the call and turned to Kais. "I'm going to find my fiancé and try to enjoy the rest of my evening. Why don't you join me?"

Kais' face was strained. He looked like he'd aged ten years in the few minutes they were in his office. "I don't know if I can. I don't think you understand what we're dealing with here."

CHAPTER 4

O livia glanced over her shoulder. Xander should have been back by now. He'd promised no work tonight. And unlike the average man, he wasn't just shuffling through some papers or staring at a computer screen. Work for him could mean something that would take him off the island or threatened his life.

Eliza rubbed her hand across Olivia's back. "I'm sure they'll be out in a few minutes. You know how Xander is—working all the time."

"Well, not all the time."

"What do you think of the house so far?"

"Your house is beautiful. I don't know why you offered it to Xander and me for our wedding. We have to pay you something for the inconvenience." Olivia held her wine glass with both hands. Eliza was a beautiful woman. She was the kind of woman that Olivia imagined appealed to Xander. Her dark, straight hair matched her dark eyes. Her skin was the color of bleached sand. Everything about her was in stark contrast to Olivia. Eliza was the sun and Olivia was the moon with curly hair, wide hips and lips so full she could cover Xander's mouth with ease. Her skin tone was closer to mahogany than alabaster. When Xander wrapped his arms around her, she couldn't help but notice his tawny complexion against her dark skin.

Eliza led her through a series of distinguished rooms, one more beautiful than the next. Each room was themed and color-coordinated to match the paintings on the walls. The smell of old money permeated the elaborate trappings purchased with new money.

"I love to entertain," Eliza said, before plucking a shrimp off a passing server's tray. "You'd be doing me a favor by letting me host such a special event. It's not often one of the island's most eligible bachelors gets married."

"How long have you known Xander?" She'd get the answers that Xander was reluctant to share.

"We go way back. I knew him from Washington." Eliza pointed to a painting on the wall. "Kais bought this for me when he asked me to marry him. It's a Monet."

"It's lovely. I love the muted colors." Olivia searched for something more to say. Her taste ran more toward bold colors and art she could touch. She didn't need museum quality pieces in her home.

A young woman entered the room with a young boy positioned on her hip. She walked up to Eliza who removed the sleepy boy from her arms.

She lifted his chin. "Can you say hello, Luc? Say hi to Olivia."

"Hey, Luc," Olivia rubbed his cheek. "Are you sleepy?"

"I wanna stay for the party," he pouted.

"It's just a bunch of old people. You'll have more fun in your room with your toys." She tried to make him smile. Olivia lost her breath again. She always did when she looked at Luc. His hair was dark like his mother's, but that was the only resemblance. His greenish-blue eyes, dark hair and ivory skin made him a miniature Xander. How was it that she was the only one who noticed the remarkable resemblance? The boy waved his pinky finger before dropping his head back on his mother's shoulder and inserting his thumb in his mouth.

"I'll come upstairs later this evening and kiss you goodnight. Okay?" Eliza kissed his forehead and handed him back to the young girl who carried him back upstairs.

"Xander will be disappointed he didn't get to see Luc." Olivia pushed the words past the lump sitting at the back of her throat. Every time she saw Luc, her reaction was the same.

"He's had a long day. At four, he'll get pretty cranky if he doesn't go to bed soon. I know I should break him from the thumb sucking, but I keep thinking there is plenty of time. I adore him." She pointed across the room. "Oh look, here come our husbands. I told you they wouldn't be too long." She guided Olivia back the way they'd come.

"Sorry, I didn't mean to be gone that long." Xander slipped his arm around her and kissed her forehead.

"Let me get us some drinks." Kais disappeared through another doorway without waiting for anyone to reply.

"Is everything okay?" Eliza asked Xander. Her hand rested on his shoulder in a way that was too familiar.

"Nothing I can't handle." He maneuvered Olivia slightly right, just away from Eliza's touch. "Let's get something to eat. We'll be back, Eliza." With his hand still around her waist, they walked in the opposite direction of Kais.

"Are you sure you're okay? You've got a funny look on your face," Xander said.

"The house is overwhelming. It's beautiful, but a lot to take in." She tightened her hold on his arm.

"Let's look at the garden." Xander maneuvered her through the door leading to the back of the house. His familiarity with the layout was noticeable. "I know you can't see all the details in the dark but imagine a reception out here. With the right caterer, it could be grand." He pointed to brick pavers. "The path there leads to a private beach."

"The wedding and reception we talked about was nothing like this. I thought we wanted something simpler. Simple elegance. Even if we raised our expectation a little, I wasn't thinking something this opulent."

"All I'm asking you to do is leave all options open. We can start to disregard some later." He pulled her into his side and kissed her forehead.

Olivia nodded, only half agreeing. Now wasn't the time to talk about the reception venue or the food choices, or the colors they'd wear, or the type of cake they'd eat. As a couple, there were more important things demanding their attention. Falling in love with Xander was easy, she needed to make sure they had the enchantment that would keep them together a lifetime.

He pulled her into his arms and swayed to a rhythm that he hummed. "Isn't this romantic?"

"Yes," she purred, pressing her body closer. "Just you and me and the moon."

"We'd better get back inside. This type of party is pretty rare on Sebastian, so let's enjoy it." He guided her back toward the dazzling palace that stirred questions but provided no answers.

CHAPTER 5

Xander opened the door for Olivia. More people had arrived in the few minutes he and Olivia had spent in the garden, but the line at the buffet table had diminished. "From the spread on the table, it looks like Kais and Eliza spared nothing."

"Yes, if they intended to impress someone tonight, they've succeeded." Olivia placed avocado slices on her plate. "What's the occasion for this party?"

"I think it's an anniversary or a birthday." Xander held a melon ball to her mouth. She bit it and nodded.

It was difficult to contain his excitement. Kais and Eliza were offering their house to them. It was the most elegant home on the island and Olivia deserved the best. If they got married in New York or D.C., a nice venue wouldn't be an issue. The offerings on Sebastian presented a challenge.

"You were in there a long time and Kais came out looking paler than when he went in. Is he okay?"

"That's a story we'll discuss later. It's business. Maybe dirty business, but I'll figure that out."

He fished his ringing phone out of his pants pocket and

held up his index finger indicating he'd only be a minute. "It's Omar. I need to take this call."

"What's up? What have you found?" he spoke into his phone.

"I think you need to get down here," Omar said. It was their code. As few details as possible were discussed on the phone.

"I'm on my way." He ended the call and turned to Olivia. "I've got to go. If you'd like to stay here, I can come back for you."

She glanced over her shoulder. "No, I don't want to stay without you."

He took Olivia's plate and handed it to a server. "We've got to go," he said, guiding her toward the door.

"Aren't you going to tell Kais and Eliza we're leaving?" Olivia had to hurry to keep up with him.

"I don't have time. I'll call tomorrow with my apologies."

Xander gnawed the inside of his cheek. There was a whole lot more going on that Kais hadn't shared. If he wasn't upfront with the details of his business, there was a reason. Kais was one of those customers that shared as little as possible. But everything had checked out during his client evaluation, so Xander didn't hesitate to take him on. He only required security for his warehouse. It was easy and the money was good.

"What is going on, Xander? You're driving like a maniac," Olivia held on to the car grab-bar above her head as he turned a corner.

"It's business. I know I promised tonight was only about looking at the Bisset house, but something's come up. I'll make it up to you."

"It's okay, but you had better slow down before you hit someone or something. You seem rattled."

"There must be trouble at the warehouse. Omar's message

was cryptic, but I know him. There was enough tension in his voice to slice through steel." He pulled to a stop beside Omar's car at the entrance to the storage complex. "I'm going to ask you to wait in the car and keep the doors locked." He placed his hand on her thigh. "If you see trouble, drive out of here and go straight home."

"You're scaring me, Xander." She latched on to his hand. "Just a few hours ago you said there was nothing dangerous going on and now I feel like we're speeding toward a catastrophe."

"Bae, I would have left you with Eliza if I thought you'd be in danger. You'll be fine here, just don't get out of the car. But just in case…do what I said."

"I'll stay here, Xander." She peered through the windshield at Omar as he approached the car. "I get it, this is your work."

He pried her hand loose, kissed her cheek, and climbed out of the car, motioning for her to lock the doors before turning to his assistant. "What the hell is going on, Omar?"

Before Omar could answer, a police car pulled up and Jimmie, the chief, stepped out.

"Okay, you two, what's so important you called me away from my wife's fried plantains?" Jimmie wore his signature khaki shorts and infamous sandals that had to cost no more than ten dollars.

"It's not good." Omar walked several steps ahead of them. At the door to the unit, he inserted a key into the lock.

"Talk to me, Omar. What's going on?" Xander demanded, his voice echoing in the night air.

"Let me get the door unlocked. The two of you can see for yourselves." He pushed the door open. The dim light inside couldn't mask the scene. At the entrance to the small storage unit were two bodies. Both were tied and bound. Each had a bullet through the front of their heads. On the concrete floor under each man was a darkened pool of blood littered with brain matter. A quick glance confirmed the unit was empty except for the bodies.

"The killer wanted them to see what was happening. Sadistic bastard." Xander pinched the bridge of his nose, studying the scene.

"Who are these guys?" Jimmie placed his arm in front of the door to block their entrance, as if they didn't know they couldn't enter the crime scene. He pulled a pair of shoe covers out of his back pocket and slipped them over his sandals. Then he pulled on a pair of latex gloves. Xander held out his hand for a pair also and slipped them on.

"They're cold. This must have happened some time ago," Jimmie said.

"I've never met Jeffrey, but this must be Kais' man. The other is one of mine—Calvin." Xander felt like a weight had been placed on his shoulders. What remained of Calvin's face was almost unrecognizable, except his curly hair. Even though blood matted the hair, Xander instantly recognized his man. Calvin hadn't worked for Fitzgerald Security Systems long, but everyone on the team knew his laid-back demeanor. "I assigned him this detail because it was easy and didn't require the expertise and precision of some of the higher profile cases. How the hell did this happen?" His voice strained. "He was only pulling security duty. How hard can it be to walk back and forth and keep everyone out? What the fuck happened here, Omar?"

"I've been here ten minutes. We'll find out." Omar pulled the door closed.

Jimmie pulled his phone from his pocket and punched in a number. "Sara, I need a forensic team at the storage facility on Peacock and get Andy out of bed and tell him to get over here." He ended the call, then pulled a notepad from his breast pocket. "Okay, Xander, give me the details."

Xander combed his fingers through his hair. Now wasn't the time to tell Jimmie everything Kais had shared with him. He needed to talk to him again tomorrow, then he'd be able to talk with the chief of police. "I don't know much." He measured his words. "We are protecting this unit for a client."

"Name?" Jimmie positioned his pen over the pad.

"How about I come down to the station tomorrow morning and talk with you? Olivia is in the car. I need to get her home." Xander backed away.

Jimmie eyed him. "Xander," he started. "I've got two murders here. This isn't one of your cases, it's one of mine. Don't try to yank a knot in my ass. I want you at the station in the morning and be ready to talk." Jimmie looked at Omar. "Where were you two tonight anyway?"

Omar shoved his hands in his pocket.

"Come on, Jimmie. You know we didn't do this. If we did, we would have cleaned up our mess and you wouldn't have known anything," said Xander. "Look at me, do I look like I was out committing murder dressed in a tux?"

"And I'm in running pants, but I'm just as shocked as you," Omar added.

Jimmie gave them half a smile. "You both answered too fast. You haven't done that before have you?"

Xander headed toward the car with Omar at his side. "You wonder, don't you?" he yelled over his shoulder at Jimmie.

"Hey, are you both leaving? I had to leave my dinner and you two get to go home?" Jimmie called to them.

Xander and Omar continued walking away. Xander waved without slowing his pace. "See you in the morning, Jimmie."

Once they were standing in front of Xander's car out of earshot, Omar stopped. Xander glanced through the windshield and saw the panic in Olivia's eyes. She started to reach for the door handle, but he held up his hand halting her.

"Let me contact Calvin's family," Omar kicked a pebble across the lot. "I know his family. I need to be the one to let them know he's not coming home tonight."

Xander eyed his assistant. After seven years of working side-by-side, he could tell Omar was fighting back emotion. This was only the second time they'd lost a team member, so there was no set protocol. But as the owner, Xander thought the responsibility was his.

"I don't want to argue about it, Xander. I need to do this. I hired Calvin. Besides, you've got Olivia in the car. By the time you drop her off, the news may have already reached his mom."

"Okay, but tell them as little as possible. I don't want a lot of rumors gathering speed. We're going to have a hard enough time finding out what's going on here."

"Yeah, I got it."

"We need to talk—you and me. I know it's late, but how about you talk to his family, grab something to eat, then give me a call." He pulled up his sleeve and glanced at his watch. "Two hours, okay? In the meantime, I'll try to reach Kais and tell him what's happened. Did you notice the unit was empty?"

"I did. What were we guarding? If it was something of value, why was it in such an inexpensive place? We could have provided a more secure place and detail."

"It was only supposed to be for a few weeks, and according to Kais, this was all he needed. He's got more explaining to do. I'll get answers, and we'll go over the details tonight."

"Who'd shoot a kid like Calvin? He wasn't even twenty-five." Omar stared at the ground, shaking his head.

"We're going to find out."

CHAPTER 6

Omar walked away with slumped shoulders. He had insisted on telling Calvin's family about his murder, but it was going to be difficult for him. The whole team would be distracted for the next few days.

Movement in the car drew Xander's attention. Olivia wasn't going to stay inside the car much longer. He motioned for her to unlock the doors and climbed inside. He turned the ignition and backed out of the lot. She was going to ask, and even though he didn't want to talk about it, he'd have to.

They hadn't gone far when Olivia smacked her hand on the dashboard. "Aren't you going to tell me what that was all about? I don't usually ask you questions about what you do or how you do it, but this happened right in front of my face. You have to say something."

He placed his hand on her knee. "The less you know, the safer you are. I'm not sure I have a handle on all of this yet. I don't have full knowledge."

"Xander, stop trying to protect me and talk. Your jaw is so tight, I can see you grinding your teeth together."

"Calvin was killed tonight."

"Calvin? Calvin? Do I know Calvin?"

He answered without looking at her, "He's only worked with us for a few months."

"That new guy?" Olivia fell back against the seat, like recalling him had taken her energy. "The one who came to our Carnival celebration?"

He nodded.

"Xander, how did this happen?" The pitch of her voice was two octaves higher, which wasn't a good sign.

"I don't know yet."

"You don't want to discuss it, but this is exactly what I was talking about earlier. Anything could happen at any time and I feel like there is nothing I can do. I have no control over our lives. I'm not a doll you need to protect."

"Talking won't bring Calvin back. I need to find out who did this and I will. Then we can talk about what's bothering you."

"Do you expect me to sit quietly until then?"

"Olivia, please give me a moment to process what has happened tonight. I just can't talk right now."

They were quiet for the remainder of the ride. Tension gathered in his shoulders. It was going to be a long night, and Kais had better be able to provide a whole lot more information.

He pulled into the drive in front of their house. Olivia stepped out of the car before he could open her door. With his hand resting on her lower back, they made their way inside. "I'm sorry about the way the night turned out. We were supposed to be checking out a wedding location. That fell apart fast, but I'll make it up to you."

She cupped his face between the palms of her hands. "Baby, you need to do what you do best. We have time to find a place." She placed her lips against his in a tender kiss. He turned it into something more aggressive, inserting his

24

tongue into her mouth and tangoing as if she was his lifeline to stability. Sending her a message of how important she was to him, every breath he took had her in it.

When she withdrew, he held onto her shoulders. His love for her burned hotter today than it did two years ago when he proposed. In the beginning, her stalling didn't seem like an issue, but days turned into months and now it was two years and she still hadn't decided. He needed to know she was in one hundred percent, tonight and always. "Omar is going to stop by later. Maybe we can have a quickie before he gets here?"

She slipped off her shoes. "Whatever you need, sweetheart."

"I need to make some calls, but God knows I don't want to miss this opportunity." He loosened his tie.

"The offer is good anytime, any day. Whenever you're ready." Her voice dropped to a seductive whisper. The one she knew was an instant turn-on, then she backed away while pushing the straps of her gown down her arms.

"I'm going into my office. Now. Because you, Ms. Olivia Sika, are a distraction. If I don't..." He turned around and headed toward his office. He never got enough of Olivia, but tonight he needed to put something ahead of her.

Behind his desk, he dialed Kais' number. His information-hiding client picked up on the first ring. "What the hell took you so long? I've been waiting for hours. You tore out of here without saying a word."

"Let me tell you how we're going to play this, Kais. I'm going to tell you what I know, then you're going to tell me what you know. No bullshit this time, I only want facts."

"You work for me, damn it. You can't talk to me that way."

"When I lose a man protecting your fucking property and I've only gotten half-assed answers, then you ought to be happy I don't get in my car, come to your house, and beat the shit out of you. Now you answer my question." Xander clenched his fist and pounded the desk. "What was in your storage unit?"

"My God, is Jeffrey dead? Oh my God. Oh my God."

"The storage unit, Kais. What was in it?" Xander's voice was firmer this time.

Through the phone, he could hear Kais huffing. "Nothing was in it. I needed to create a distraction. I just wanted everyone to think something was there. I don't trust anyone."

"Okay, then why is Jeffrey and my man, Calvin dead over an empty unit? If they didn't find what they were looking for tonight, don't you think they will continue to look?"

"I've got that painting in a safe place. They won't find it."

"Who are they? And don't give me that bullshit about you don't know. Tell me what you do know. You had to have a way to communicate with this anonymous buyer and a way to transfer funds between the two of you."

"I call him LC. That's it. We communicate by cell phones. He wired money to me. To my account."

"Then you know what account the money came from. Give me the account numbers."

"Look, Xander, I'm not going to give account numbers over the phone. We can meet tomorrow and talk."

"Now you're saying you don't trust me either."

"How do I know my phone isn't tapped? Or my house wired?"

"Is that a possibility?"

"How the hell do I know? Anything is possible, right? According to you, two men are dead."

CHAPTER 7

I n the bedroom, Olivia put her book down and pushed open the French doors leading to the balcony. She could spend hours peering over the railing, listening to the quiet rush of water from the beach. The salty smell of the ocean had a calming effect. The moon seemed to rest on the horizon like a large, white beach ball. If she wasn't so exhausted, she'd grab her camera and take some pictures. Down the hill, the silhouette of the rental house was visible. There was no way she could look at that place and not think about how it had brought her and Xander together. Back then, she'd been terrified someone wanted to kill her, and Xander had been the one to assist her.

No matter how much time went by, she couldn't get used to the idea that danger always lurked around the corner of Xander's life. His occupation was hazardous and the more thrilling it was, the more he seemed to like it. He worked from the house, but seldom was she aware of any of his activity, so tonight had her anxious. She'd been at the crime scene and after what happened with Ajay, she'd vowed never to be vulnerable or afraid again.

Xander walked into the bedroom. "You waited up for me?"

She turned to face him. "Yeah. I figured you might want to talk."

"I just finished talking to Omar." He kicked off his shoes and grabbed her hand. With his arms around her waist, they stared into the night. She could feel him relaxing. The inky black water was only noticeable where the moon shined on it.

"I was thinking about how we met," she said.

"Our butting heads at the airport wasn't romantic. I thought you were going to bite me."

She nudged him. "Not that part. I like to think we actually met that morning you startled me on the beach."

He was quiet for a moment. "You tell the story your way and I tell it mine. I noticed you at the airport. I knew then you were a sexy spitfire that I wanted to know better. And it's been worth every single minute."

"You're just saying that because you want sex tonight."

"I'm saying that because it's true. The sex part is also true." He turned her and stared at her face. Something was on his mind and if he followed his usual path, it wouldn't be long before he shared it with her. She just hoped he didn't want to talk about the wedding or a date.

She pushed up on her toes and inserted her tongue into his mouth. Sure, she was delaying the wedding conversation and she couldn't give him a logical reason why. She unbuckled his belt, then slipped her hand inside his briefs. His moan said wedding talk might be delayed tonight. At least for a few hours.

He helped her out of her nightgown and cupped her breasts before leading her to the lounger on the balcony. She pulled down his pants, leaving them in a pile, and then ran her hand along his muscular abdomen and legs. He'd tattooed her name just above his hip bone. She loved running her finger across the blue engraving. She had promised to tattoo his name just above her breast, but at the last minute she chickened out. She couldn't convince Xander it was because of the pain and not because she didn't want to commit.

"You like that, don't you?" he asked.

"I love it. No one has ever done something like this for me." With her index finger, she outlined the 'O' in her name.

"I'd do anything for you." He climbed on top of her. His enlarged shaft pressed against her thigh when he buried his head into the curve of her neck. The kisses started out tender and moist, and then grew in intensity.

The location of the house on the hill gave them complete privacy. She couldn't count the number of times they'd made love outdoors, something she'd never thought possible when she lived in New York. A gentle breeze crossed the balcony, but it did little to cool her warm skin.

She shifted her hips to manage his muscular frame. With her hand caressing his neck, she planted kisses there before moving to his chest, and then his stomach. When she reached his penis, she slowed. Taking it into her mouth and running her tongue along the ridge, something about the way he smelled excited her. The way he tasted was as satisfying as the way he touched her. He filled all the empty places, rounding them out and making her whole. After two years of nightly lovemaking, her body always reacted as if it was the first time, exciting and new.

He arched his back and dug his fingers into her thick hair. She teased him until he repeated her name in a voice so husky it was hard to make out.

"Olivia, I can't stop," His body spasmed with gratification, then he nudged her up and scooped her into his arms, carrying her into the house. "You don't play fair," he said before easing her onto the bed.

"Everything I do is about pleasing you." She wiggled higher in the bed.

"I feel the same way." He buried his head between her legs. The moment his mouth touched her, the heat seared pleasure throughout her body. Her soul surrendered to him, the way it always did. She needed to convince her mind that marriage wouldn't end the good thing they had. It would only enhance their relationship.

Xander's movements were slow, tender, and intense. He played her body like it was an instrument that belonged to him. As independent as she was, with Xander, there was never any doubt he controlled every situation and the bedroom was no different. Her body tensed as every fiber yielded to him, gathering in her core. She clamped her thighs around his head and lifted her hips off the bed. There was no need to say anything he had to know what he was doing to her and how good it felt. When her orgasm rocked her body, the only thing she could do was tremble in ecstasy.

He slowed his assault on her body, allowing her to enjoy the cascading euphoria. Then he climbed on top of her and buried his penis deep inside of her. She wrapped her legs around his waist and drew him in deeper, allowing him to fill her, leaving no room for questions or doubt. He was the one, her heart knew it. But her mind needed to catch up. Together, they found their rhythm and danced their own private waltz. She found his lips and drew his tongue into her mouth. They became one as the rest of the world and her fear faded away.

Early the next morning, when the sun had only tipped over the horizon and the bedroom glowed with a hint of light, Xander climbed out of bed and closed the balcony door.

"Why are you up?" Olivia stirred, pushing up in the bed.

He came to sit on her side of the bed. "I can't sleep."

She rubbed his lower back. The tension in his muscles was noticeable, the skin unforgiving under her touch. "Are you thinking about Calvin?"

"You know I love you, don't you?" he asked.

She was fully awake now, swinging her feet off the bed to sit beside him. "Of course, I do. What brought this on?"

He buried his face in his hands. His breathing was regular, but she could hear each breath. "We've been together two years and engaged almost that long. We've talked about the wedding and what we're going to do when we're married, but you refuse to set the date."

Her chest tightened. All conversations led to the same place, the same complicated conversation. Of course, Xander was getting tired of the delays. They should have gone to the Justice of the Peace before either of them had too much time to think or create excuses.

When she didn't reply, he continued. "I think we're good together. You seem happy. I know I'm happy. You need to tell me what's going on. I don't want to spend any more time guessing. If you don't want to marry me, I can learn to accept that. But I've never lied to you. I want a family and kids, not a long-term girlfriend."

All the words to rebut him gathered in her throat. She'd procrastinated long enough. It was time to open up to the man she loved with her heart and soul. Xander was as bull-headed as her father. If she could handle her dad, she could handle Xander. "I want the same things and I want them with you, but I'm afraid. I've worked hard to be independent. With a family like mine, it was a difficult fight, and even more challenging to hold on to. Just before meeting you, my father was demanding I leave New York and move back to Philly." She fluffed the back of her hair, knowing it had flattened overnight. "You have this dangerous career and you're always protecting me. It would be so easy for me to fall behind your shadow. I don't know how to be your wife and still be true to myself."

He jumped off the bed. "What the hell are you talking about, Olivia? I've never smothered you. You have your career, traveling all over the world without me. I've never questioned any of your decisions or choices. That sounds like a load of crap."

She stood and faced him. "Take me to the driving range today."

"What about your work? You're a photographer. I don't see the connection." There was an edge in his voice.

"My work has nothing to do with going to the range. I don't understand why you're fighting me on this. I put part of my career on hold to live here on Sebastian with you, but I want to know that no matter what, I can protect myself without you." She pounded her chest. "I need to do this for me."

"Honey, not everything is clean cut. There are times when I have to get dirty, play dirty. I'm always on the right side of the law, but sometimes I'm inches away from legal, and for those times, I have good lawyers and even better connections to keep me out of jail. I don't want that for you. If something happens, I'll handle it."

Before she could respond, he marched into the bathroom and slammed the door. "That didn't go as planned," she mumbled while climbing back into bed. "That wasn't a bunch of bull, Xander. I meant every word." She yelled at him.

"Yeah, well you should have told me that before I bought that expensive ring."

"Why, would you have changed your mind?" She kicked her legs like a child having a tantrum.

He didn't reply. The sound of the shower halted their

conversation. Maybe that was best or they might end up saying things they couldn't retract.

His cell phone chimed from the bedside table. Instinctively, she reached for it to silence the noise. When she saw Eliza's name her stomach somersaulted. There was something about that woman that wasn't as it appeared. She was friendly, but behind her smiling face was a woman Olivia didn't trust.

She accepted the call. "Eliza, don't you think it's a little early—"

"I really need to talk to Xander. Is he there?" Her words were terse.

"Good morning, Eliza," Olivia wouldn't be bullied.

"Yes, of course. Good morning. Is Xander there? This is an emergency. I need to speak to him." Her voice hitched.

Olivia walked across the room and rapped on the bathroom door before opening it. Xander stood in front of the mirror toweling off. "Eliza's on the phone. She needs to speak to you. It sounds important."

"You answered my phone?" He lifted his brow.

"It was disturbing my attempt to be angry with you." She held the phone out to him and made her way back to the bed just in case Eliza wanted to seduce Xander into coming to her rescue. Instead of covering her nakedness, Olivia stretched on top of the bed. If he was going to talk to another woman, at least he'd get a clear shot of what he already had.

CHAPTER 8

Xander secured the towel around his waist before putting the phone to his ear. "Eliza, what's up?"

"It's Kais. He's not here, and I don't know where he is." The words tumbled out so fast, he had to take a moment to process what she'd said.

"So why are you calling me? I'm sure he'll be there soon. We have an appointment this morning."

"No, I don't think you understand. Last night after the party, he was in his office and said he was coming to bed in a few minutes. I was so exhausted, I fell asleep. He never came to bed. This morning, he's gone. His car is here, but he's not. I've looked." She sounded frantic.

"Maybe he went for a walk."

"Kais doesn't walk. You know that. He drives down the lane to collect the mail. He didn't get that gut from walking or working out. Kais never leaves the house unless he's in that expensive car. The light is still on in his office. It looks like he stepped away for a moment. What did the two of you talk about last night?"

"I'll come over." He gazed at Olivia with her legs spread wide. She was taunting him, and it was working.

"No, I want to know right now. Tell me." Eliza was almost screaming.

"I'll be there in ten minutes." He ended the call and placed his hand on his hip as he walked into the bedroom. "Really, Bae?"

"Is it working?"

"It always works." He climbed across the bed, stopping long enough to kiss her before exiting on the opposite side. He yanked open a drawer and started to dress.

"Where are you going? We're in the middle of an argument," Olivia demanded from the bed.

"I've got to go see Eliza." He pulled on his jeans.

"She calls and you're going to run out of here just like that? What does that woman have over you?"

He tugged on a t-shirt. "It's work, Olivia. That's all this is, work. There is nothing between me and Eliza." He bent over her and kissed her forehead.

"If you're going to run out to another woman at least kiss me like you want to come back to me." Her eyes. It was always her eyes that stopped him cold, drew him in, and held her in his heart.

"You have got to be the most independent woman I know. Why you'd worry about losing something coded in your DNA, I'll never understand." He slipped his hand behind her neck and thrust his tongue in her mouth. The need to claim her the way she claimed him was more powerful this morning than ever. He didn't want to pull away, but he had to. "When I come home, we're going to finish our conversation."

"It wasn't a conversation. It was a disagreement."

She grabbed him around the neck and kissed him one more time. Damn, for a man that wasn't going to get caught up, he hadn't done very well. He'd wait until she was ready to marry him, he just wouldn't tell her. Not yet.

"Be careful," she yelled as he walked out of the bedroom.

"I always am. Except when it came to you."

He arrived at Eliza's house within ten minutes as promised. She opened the door before he turned off the ignition. The wild look in her eyes wasn't a good sign. "What took you so long?"

"Let's go inside and talk."

Eliza's eyes darted around the lush landscape of her estate as if she expected to see Kais materialize in the garden. Xander closed the car door and hurried behind her toward the house. "Look at his office. I haven't touched a thing. He wouldn't have left it this way."

"I was supposed to meet with Kais this morning. I called him last night, he was going to give me some information on an art deal. I think this is the stuff we talked about." He pushed the papers aside.

"You talked to him last night?"

"He didn't tell you? That's odd."

"I told you. I was tired after the party, so I went right to bed." Her eyes dropped to the floor long enough to let him know she wasn't telling the full truth. "We don't have secrets. We share everything."

"Then you know about the missing piece of art?"

"What are you talking about? There aren't any pieces missing. We run a reputable business. If we've been commissioned to find a piece or sell a piece, we do it. Nothing goes missing." The pitch of her voice certainly said she believed what she was saying.

"Do you have any cameras surveying the property?"

"No, of course not. This isn't New York. Who needs that? Do you have surveillance cameras surrounding your house?"

He didn't. This was Sebastian Island. Crime was almost

non-existent on the island. At least it was until last night. In his line of work, he kept a close watch on his house, but very few people knew that. "Is it possible that Kais is having an affair or that he left you?"

Eliza rubbed her eyes. "How can I answer that question? I don't think he's having an affair. Our relationship is fine. I don't believe…I don't think he's having an affair," she seemed to muster the energy to make the proclamation.

"I'm not trying to upset you. I'm just eliminating the obvious."

"He wouldn't leave and not take some of his things. Besides, he adores Luc. If he was going to leave me, he'd try to take Luc with him."

The thought of Luc not being on the island made Xander wince. "Did he tell you about the shooting last night at the storage unit?"

She covered her mouth and her eyes opened wider. "Shooting? He didn't say anything, but like I said, we didn't talk after the party. Was anyone hurt?"

"Two men were killed. Jeffrey and a member of my team, Calvin."

"Jeffrey? Jeffrey Sager? Are…are…you sure?" She clutched at her throat with one hand and steadied herself on the desk with the other. Tears formed in her eyes. "What happened? How could Kais keep this from me?" Looking bewildered, Eliza struggled to get to a chair and sit.

"Do you need something? A glass of water?"

She pulled a tissue from the box on the desk and wiped her eyes as sobs took over.

"So, there were some secrets between you?" Xander asked when she seemed to pull herself together.

She nodded her agreement. "I'm sure he would have told me this morning."

Xander strolled behind the desk and glanced at the

papers. There were several sticky notes pasted on top of typed pages. One had the initials LC and a bunch of numbers. Xander extracted his cell phone from his pocket and snapped a picture of the document. He took several more pictures. "How much did you know about Kais' business?"

"What are you doing?" Eliza stood and moved closer to the desk, coming to stand beside him. "We run the business together. I know everything." She snatched open the top desk drawer. "Look, his wallet is here. Why would he leave and not take his money and identification?"

"Where is his cell?"

"I don't know. I've dialed it all morning. He's not picking up."

The computer on Kais' desk was on, but the screen saver swirled around the monitor, displaying nothing.

"Do you know what the initials LC stand for?" He pointed at the note.

"No."

"Do you know where the painting is that LC was buying from your company?"

"I can look through my files."

"Do you know who the artist is on this elusive piece?"

She shrugged. "When I said we run the business together, I didn't mean all the minutia. Some of the little details I work out and some he works out. I can show you what we have in inventory."

"Do you know the password to this computer?"

"No."

"Can you get into the business accounts?"

Her head snapped back. "Of course. What are you getting at, Xander?"

"I'm asking questions. I don't want to take anything for

granted. Everyone operates a little different." He touched her elbow. "Let's go log onto your computer."

She led the way out of the room. "What do you think you'll find?"

"I want a list of customers—name and contact information that bought or sold art in the last year. I want to see the business calendar. I also want to know where you store artwork while you're finalizing a transaction and account numbers. And anything else you can share."

They walked to the opposite end of the house. Her heeled slippers clapped against the marble floors as they made their way to her office. It was more ornate than Kais'. Where his was all walnut furniture and stuffed bookshelves, her office was chrome and glass and pink. Xander pulled out the modern acrylic chair behind her desk and peered over her shoulder.

She clicked through the computer keys quickly and printed out the pages he indicated. When they finished, he placed the chair back and leaned over the desk, pressing his palms on the surface. "When you came downstairs this morning, nothing was out of order, right?"

"Xander, please stop asking me so many questions. I'm already agitated, and your questions just make things sound more sinister."

"I'm hoping something I've asked will trigger your memory, that's all."

Her eyes grew round to match the shape of her mouth. She started to speak, but no words came out.

"So, I was right when I said the two of you don't share everything. There are some business details you don't know about. Some pretty important ones."

She jumped up. Her body was rigid as her eyes turned cold. "You couldn't wait to prove me wrong, could you? You wanted to find something wrong with Kais. Why do you dislike him? He didn't come between us. We both knew what we had wasn't going to last. You were rebounding for God's sake. All you could do was mope about what's-her-face. What does it matter anyway, you're engaged now, so why can't you let it go?" she screamed at him, swiping the tears from her cheeks.

He circled the desk and wrapped his arms around Eliza.

"You bastard," she said without trying to shake him off. "Where is Kais? Where is he?"

"We'll find him, Eliza. Try to calm down." He patted her back. "Is Luc here? I'd like to see him."

"Yes, he's still sleeping. He'll be up soon." She pulled away.

"Don't wake him. I'll see him the next time I stop over. Try to stay calm, so he doesn't get upset. Act normal when he comes down. Let me do some looking around. I'll call you later today. Okay?"

It took a while for her to respond. "He's a good man, Xander, and you were never going to marry me."

"I don't dislike Kais. I think he plays things loose and fast, and I think you could have done better. But if you're happy, that's all that matters. Plus, you've got Luc, the sweetest little boy on the whole island." He walked out without giving her a chance to say anything more.

From his car, he dialed Omar. "Meet me at the house."

"I don't have any answers yet. It's only been a few hours. What's up?" Omar asked.

"Something else has come up. And I've got a bad feeling."

CHAPTER 9

Olivia heard Xander enter the house. She placed her camera on the desk before leaving her studio to greet him. They needed to finish the conversation from this morning. From across the room, the coral smudge of Eliza's lipstick was visible on his shirt. Not on the collar in the stereotypical place, but on his chest... too close to his heart.

"Is everything okay?" She kissed him. Her heart revved the way it always did when they connected, but her brain swam in jealousy. Eliza was like a ghost flying around their relationship, touching off her insecurities.

"No. Something is wrong, but I don't have any details. Not yet."

"But you've got lipstick on your shirt." She pointed.

He looked down and tried to brush it away. "Yeah, I tried to console Eliza."

"Isn't that what her husband is for?"

"He's missing. And I don't think he's out for a morning walk." The worry lines on his forehead deepened.

"You're doing missing persons now?"

"No, but..."

"Why didn't she call the police instead of you?"

He pulled her into his chest and held her tight. "Bae, she is just...she just called me first. It doesn't mean anything."

"It does to me, but I'm glad you're home."

He held her at arm's length. "Olivia, you're being silly. I don't have feelings for Eliza, and she has none for me. Believe me."

Omar knocked on the door, interrupting her chance to respond.

"I've got some work to do. We'll be in my office." Together, they walked away, leaving her standing in the foyer. She hadn't even greeted Omar.

She spun around to follow them but stopped. This is what she feared. Love changed people, but not her. She wouldn't become one of those women who was so in love with a man she stepped away from who she was. Nor did she want to rely on Xander to make her whole.

She returned to her studio to collect her camera and her accessory bag. The phone interrupted her escape to the beach. Her girlfriend, Eva's number showed on the display. She lifted the receiver.

"I'm glad I caught you. I've found the perfect place for your wedding. This hall has everything. You'll love it." Eva's voice bubbled like expensive champagne.

Only Eva could make her forget her anger. "Did I ask you to look for a place for me?"

"No, but isn't that what friends do for friends?"

"We haven't set a date." Olivia settled into the chair behind the desk. The anger that had sat on her chest dissolved.

"Well, this location is so fabulous, you'll set a date within ten minutes of looking at the pictures. I've sent you a link. Please look at it."

"I told you we want to get married here on Sebastian."

"And I told you this place will make you change your mind." Eva insisted.

"Eva, slow down. I'm not ready to set a date. I don't know when I will be."

"Has something happened?" Eva's voice changed to soft and caring.

"Marriage works for you and David. You guys make it seem easy. But I'm an independent woman. I'm not ready to give that up."

"Oh, you think I'm not independent. Do you think I'm subservient to David?" she huffed.

"No. No. That's not what I meant." She shook her head. "I'm not sure marriage is for me."

"Marriage isn't like a pair of shoes, Olivia. It can be for everyone, if they are open. It's about love and nothing more." Eva made everything sound easy. Life for her fell into place. But for Olivia, it was always a jigsaw puzzle, and she was certain some pieces were missing.

The line was silent for several beats. She had no response to give Eva. Nothing trumped the simple love Eva described. "Today he came home with lipstick on his shirt. I told you about Eliza; that woman is shady. Do you know how close she had to get to leave her lipstick on his shirt?" Her voice was taut.

"Do you think he's cheating on you?"

"That's not the point. I should trust him enough to not care. Instead, I'm playing out scenarios in my head. I've never been a jealous person, but Eliza has me thinking crazy."

"Maybe that's because you love him so much. Is it possible, you didn't care enough about anyone until now?"

Leave it to Eva to lean toward reason. Sometimes, she wanted her friend to be bat-shit-crazy with her. "He promised to take me to the shooting range so I can protect myself. He's found a reason to delay every time I bring it up. I feel like during the day we live two different lives and at night we become one. One of his men was killed the other day."

"That's probably why he wants to keep you away from that part of his life."

"How do you do it with David? Knowing every day his life could—"

"I don't think about that stuff, Olivia. When I'm with him, I make sure he knows how much I love him, and we cherish our time together. That's what's important."

"I can't sit on the side and wait and hope he comes home every night. I don't know if I have what it takes to be that kind of wife or if that's the life I want."

Eva sucked in a deep breath. "Maybe you're not ready to get married. It sounds like you and Xander still have stuff to work out."

They were very different. Olivia could never accept half the things Eva was willing to put up with from David – the long hours, the uncertainty if he'd come home.

"Olivia, promise you'll at least think about some of the things I've said. Be honest with Xander. He'll understand. The man loves you."

"I'll promise if you promise not to hassle me about setting a date. I'm getting enough of that from Xander."

"Deal."

They ended the call and Olivia scooped up her camera. The tension pressing on her shoulders wouldn't ease until she was looking at the world through the lens of her camera.

CHAPTER 10

Omar settled into the chair across the desk from Xander with the same grim look from the night before.

"Are you doing okay, Omar?" Xander asked. Omar was more than an assistant. He was like a brother, the person he turned to when he needed to talk and tease out solutions. His trust in Omar never faltered. There were no secrets between them.

"I can't get over how Calvin's mother broke down. She was inconsolable, and this morning, I got a call this morning from his sister. They don't have money for a funeral." Omar rubbed his forehead.

"Tell them Fitzgerald Security will cover all the funeral expenses. They shouldn't have to worry about something like this now." Xander held Omar's gaze, making sure his sentiment was received.

Omar only nodded.

"Eliza called this morning. She says Kais is missing. Just disappeared. Didn't say goodbye, and he left the house without taking his car or wallet."

"What do you think that means?" Omar shifted forward in the chair. Distracted by this turn of events, the gloom disappeared from his face.

"I'm guessing, but I think he didn't intend to go away for long. Maybe he went for a walk through the gardens, or someone or something lured him out of the house."

"Makes sense, but where is he now? Wouldn't he call Eliza? He must know she'd worry."

"I'll call Jimmie when we're done here and see if he can help us track him down." Xander spread the documents he'd gathered from Eliza on the table. "This is the information Eliza gave me. According to her, their regular warehouse is in the commercial district. And this is a list of the items they have in inventory. She had these pictures of the most expensive items." He pushed the papers toward Omar. "I've sent someone to verify the items are still there."

Omar whistled. "This stuff looks expensive."

"Expensive enough to get two people murdered. I've already asked Jaysa to go through the client list and recent transactions. She promised to have information for us later today. Kais was worried about someone with the initials LC. This list doesn't have anyone who comes close, but she'll do a cross check. Maybe we'll get lucky."

"Eliza have any idea what happened at the storage unit last night?"

"No, she knew nothing about it. She was distraught when I told her. No matter what she says though, she and Kais had some secrets. That's evident." Xander pointed to Omar. "Now tell me what you've been able to find out."

Xander watched as Omar pulled his well-beaten notepad from his pants pocket and flipped through several pages. Whatever he was about to share, Xander's assistant didn't need to refer to his notes. The notebook was for show, but

Xander knew Omar thought the gesture made him look prepared. "I think I might be able to get a lead on this guy LC. I don't think he has any direct ties on the island, but if there is any criminal activity on the island then someone at the pool hall in the quarter knows about it. A lot of small-time criminals hang out there. The hall is the genesis of petty crime activity."

"Murder isn't a petty crime. What happened to Calvin was a professional hit."

"But I'll bet it was talked about in that pool hall."

"We can check it out later today. Any luck with the security footage from the storage facility or the surrounding area?" Xander asked.

Omar pulled a small jump drive from his shirt pocket. "The footage is grainy, but let's pull it up on your computer." He inserted the drive in the computer, tapped a few keys on the keyboard and waited.

They stared at the darkened screen for a full minute as Calvin walked back and forth, smoking and talking on his cell. Nothing about his behavior said professional, but nothing seemed threatening either.

"Fast forward to where the action starts."

Omar held up a hand. "Be patient, things will pick up in a second."

A dark sedan pulled into view and a man stepped out from the driver's side.

"Do you know who that is?" Xander pointed at the screen.

"That's Kais' man, Jeffrey. The one killed along with Calvin."

"Can we do anything to improve this graphic?"

"Negative."

"What happened to the car Jeffrey arrived in? It wasn't there last night when we arrived."

"You've never been fun to watch a movie with. Can you sit and let this unfold?"

Xander took a deep breath. They could save time if Omar just told him what he wanted to know. But Xander knew Omar always wanted to dole out the details for as long as he could after all his hard work. Xander turned his attention back to the computer.

Calvin opened the unit and allowed the man to enter, then he followed. The two men were inside for less than a minute when Calvin came out carrying a box. Jeffrey followed close behind carrying a box as well. Jeffrey fumbled for his key, and then they placed the boxes into the trunk of Jeffrey's car.

"Stop the film," Xander demanded. "Calvin didn't follow protocol. Did you see him look at any documentation?"

"Maybe they reviewed the paperwork inside the unit." Omar offered. "I know he shouldn't have unlocked the unit without seeing the paperwork first, but the kid was still learning."

"Not an excuse, Omar." Xander's voice was firm. "Were there any videos from inside the unit?"

"They were stolen. Jimmie confirmed that this morning."

"How did you get the footage?"

"Sweet talked Jimmie."

"Any idea what's in those boxes?"

"None," Omar said. "Can I start the video again? We're getting to the good part."

Xander waved his hand.

Before Jeffrey could get back into his car, another car pulled into view. Two muscular men stepped out, each holding a gun. The footage was too grainy to determine the make of the weapons. From the way they carried themselves, they looked like professional hit men. Both Calvin and his companion dropped their weapons on the ground and held their hands up. They were escorted into the unit. After a moment, two more boxes were placed in the trunks by one of the new arrivals. Calvin and Jeffrey weren't seen again. In the darkened film, two dull flashes of light popped from inside the unit. "Gunfire?" Xander asked.

Omar nodded.

The two muscular men walked out and locked the unit door. One got behind the wheel of each car and drove off.

"Somehow they did all that without showing their faces. They must have known about the cameras. But I identified the car make and model. I even got a partial plate." Omar pulled a sheet of paper from the back of his pad and unfolded it onto the center of the desk.

Xander examined the picture of the car. The photograph of the men didn't reveal much – two men dressed in black with dark hair and shoulders broad enough to stop a train. "Professionals, no doubt." Xander ran his index finger along the bridge of his nose. "I don't like that Calvin didn't follow procedure. It was almost as if these two guys waited. Like they knew what was going down tonight. Do you think Calvin was on the take?"

Omar started to speak but stopped.

"Think about it, Omar. He opens the unit without seeing any paperwork. He even helps load a box in the car."

"But without confirmation from Kais, we don't know what really happened or what was said. Don't jump to conclusions."

"I thought we were guarding paintings. Kais told me last night the unit was a decoy. He said the unit was empty, which leaves me with more questions. There had to be something of value in those boxes, or why would those two muscle guys bother taking two more boxes and driving off with them?"

"When we find Kais, we'll get answers."

"Yeah, but he's acting squirrelly. I bet he'll give us a bunch of bullshit." Xander stood and stretched his arms over his head. "It's time to do some legwork. Let's get out of here."

CHAPTER 11

Olivia had hundreds of pictures of the beach and the ocean and the waves, but there were never enough. The peacefulness of the photos eased the angst in her soul. Through the lens of the camera, there wasn't a problem she couldn't fix by changing the lens or adjusting the focus. Too bad life didn't sort out as easily.

The waves brushed her feet as she snapped pictures of a school of iridescent fish.

No matter how comforting, she couldn't spend the whole day taking pictures that she wasn't getting paid to take. She hadn't gotten that creative yet where people bought her photos as framed art.

With a sigh, she backed out of the water and sunk her toes in the sand. It was time to start home. She paused long enough to take a few shots of the Macklemore house.

She pulled at the elastic on her tank top to get air circulating near her skin. The stroll up the hill was a struggle in the afternoon heat, but the photos of the Macklemore house had been worth the stop. Every time she saw the house, it took her back to her first adult visit to Sebastian Island, the mix-up with Xander, and the first time they made love. It was her own fairy tale and reliving it always made her smile.

Maybe she was feeling melancholy. Before a wedding, a couple was supposed to be closer than ever, but her hesitancy was pushing them apart. If she didn't have a conversation with Xander, things weren't going to get much better. She was smart enough to know that, but she couldn't find the words to convey her feelings. He loved his work. Nothing she said would change that, and she didn't want to ask him to choose because she might lose.

Approaching the house, she saw Omar's car still parked in the lane. Until she had Xander alone, there would not be any meaningful conversations. She tucked her camera bag on her shoulder and made her way to the front door. Xander opened the door before she could reach for the knob. Omar stood behind him.

"Omar, I'm sorry I didn't speak sooner. You guys were in a hurry." She gave him a hug. "So, who is the lucky woman this week?" It was a running joke between them. Omar was the island playboy. With his dark good looks, women never left him alone.

"It's not like that, Olivia." Omar looked down at his feet. "I'm not looking for forever like you two. I have friends."

Xander chuckled. "That's his way of saying nobody wants to hang around here too long."

Omar huffed. "Don't assume monogamy is what everyone wants just because you two stumbled together." He walked down the stairs, leaving her and Xander alone.

"You're heading out?" she asked.

Xander kissed her on the mouth. "Yeah, we've got things to check out. I shouldn't be gone long."

"Can we talk for a moment?" She shielded her eyes from the glare of sunlight.

Xander signaled to Omar before following her inside the house. "What's up, Bae?"

"I'm going to make an appointment at the shooting range this evening. You can come with me or not, it's up to you. I've waited for you and all you've given me are excuses. After that, I'd like to go out for dinner. What time will you be back?" She pretended to be busy putting away her camera equipment so she wouldn't have to see the reaction on his face.

"I'm not sure how long we'll be out. What's going on with you?" He grabbed her arm.

"Nothing. We talked about doing this. I'm tired of waiting."

"But, why does it have to happen today? I'll take you to the range."

"Xander, it's happening today." She pulled away and put her hands on her hips. "We've debated this for months. It's something I want to do and I'm not waiting another day. If you don't want to do it, then I'll do it on my own. My father taught me to shoot a gun with some precision, I just want to get better. When Eliza called this morning, you were out of the house in five minutes. But me," she thumped her chest. "I have to wait." She hated the jealously that intertwined her words and hated even more the feeling of being second or third on his list of priorities. His work consumed him. How could she even think about getting married when every case was more important than the promises he made to her?

He pushed his lips to one side. A sure sign he didn't like her approach. "Does it have to be today?"

"Why? Are you still working on Eliza's issue?"

"It's business, Olivia."

She tilted her head. "It's always something, Xander. If you can't fit me into your busy schedule, you should tell me now before we go any further down this road. Maybe this isn't the time for us to talk about marriage. If I'm begging for your time now, it will only get worse."

"Okay, Olivia." He used her name, another sign he wasn't enjoying the conversation. "Make the shooting range appointment for six." He glanced at his watch. "I'll be back by then."

She stepped closer to him and wrapped her arms around his waist. "I don't like it when we fuss at each other."

"Then stop fussing."

CHAPTER 12

Omar pulled into a parking space a block away from the pool hall and shut off the engine. "How are we going to play this?" he asked.

"You aren't expecting trouble, are you?" Xander asked.

"I always expect trouble, that way I'm never surprised." He pulled his gun from the holster on his hip and checked the chamber. "I know you think you're a regular on the island now, but this part of town doesn't get many strait-laced Caucasians unless they want something, and it isn't usually information. It's drugs."

Xander shifted his position on the seat. Being in control was the only thing he knew, and this was the second time today someone had challenged him. First Olivia, now Omar. "I'm not new at this. I can handle myself." He pushed the door open and climbed out. "You got the devices?"

Omar patted his pocket. "The high-tech stuff. If he says something, this baby will pick it up."

"I'll make sure you get the chance to install them. I want one in the restroom too."

"How did I know that?" Omar shot him a half-smile.

Even though the sun was high in the sky, the inside of the pool hall managed to be dark. Everyone turned around to peer at them when they walked in. Two of the four billiard tables in the spacious room were being used. Wood paneling adorned all the walls, and the linoleum floor was worn through in spots. The men at the table appeared non-threatening, a bunch of retirees wasting away the afternoon. They didn't look like they could remember their last meal, no one would guess they knew anything about criminal activity. A small bar positioned at the back of the room had six bar stools and only one patron nursing the remains of his drink. The atmosphere went from friendly to freezing as all action and conversation halted.

Xander made his way across the room with Omar behind him. They took a seat on the stools at one end of the bar.

"What can I get for you?" the bartender asked in an unfriendly tone. His deep brown face was marked with lines of age. His shirt had the name Ed scripted on the pocket. He pushed two wrinkled napkins in front of them.

"Hey, Ed. I'll have a whiskey," Xander said, a little too friendly based on the look Ed gave him.

Omar opted for the same thing. They nursed their drinks while the bartender made sure he stayed as far away from them as he could.

"I'm not sitting here all day paying for overpriced cheap whiskey while the bartender won't even look our way," Xander muttered to Omar after several minutes.

"I told you not to expect a warm welcome."

"Let's get this done. Are you ready?" Xander pushed off his barstool and walked toward the bartender.

Omar spun off the stool and headed toward the bathroom.

"Ed, I think you can help me. I'm looking for some information."

Ed was slow to turn around. "What can I get you?"

Xander pushed the picture of the two men from the security footage across the bar in his direction. Before looking at the piece of paper, Ed eyed the men at the pool tables. "I know this isn't a good photo, but I've got it from a good source that you might be able to identify the men in this picture."

Ed glanced at the picture for a second before pushing it back toward Xander. "No. Can't help you."

Xander showed him the picture of the car. "How about this car, do you recognize it?"

With an annoyed look, Ed studied the piece of paper. "Man, it's a black sedan. Do you know how many black cars there are on the island? Shit, I own a black sedan." He shoved the paper toward Xander so hard it almost flew off the bar.

"Are you sure? Take another look."

"Don't need to. I can't help you. Do you want another drink?" He turned his back. "If you don't want a drink or to play a game of pool, maybe you and your buddy need to leave."

Xander looked at Omar with a raised brow. When Omar signaled, Xander followed Omar out the door. Away from the entrance, he turned to Omar. "Did you get them in place?"

"Sure did. Now all we need to do is listen and wait. Did you learn anything?" Omar asked.

"Nothing."

Xander's cell rang. He pulled it from his pocket to see Jimmie's number on the screen. "What can I do for you, Jimmie? I know I was supposed to stop by today and I will." Xander winced. He'd promised Olivia he would be home by six.

"I think I've got information you'll be interested in."

"Cool. What is it?"

"In person. Meet me at Alameda and Bleeker." Jimmie talked fast.

"That's near the east end of the beach. Why there?"

"Come now, Xander, it's important." Jimmie disconnected the call.

"What's up?" Omar asked as they climbed in the car.

"It looks like we're going to the east end. Alameda. At least we're in the neighborhood. It's what, five minutes from here?" Xander asked.

Omar put the car in gear and pulled out of the parking space. Within minutes, three squad cars and a ribbon of yellow police tape greeted them. Xander's heartbeat quickened. His first thought was Olivia. Always Olivia. But she was on the opposite side of the island.

"I don't have a good feeling about this," Omar spoke low before turning off the car.

Xander couldn't find words. He hopped out the car and rushed to find Jimmie, who stood off to the side typing into his phone. "Jimmie, tell me why you called me down here," Xander called to the police chief as he approached.

Jimmie shook his head and waved to Xander and Omar to follow him. "This way." They made their way up the sand dune and through a patch of water reeds before stopping near the shallow water.

The perspiration on his back thickened. No matter what, this would not end well. They certainly weren't here to fish, but Jimmie needing to keep the reason a secret had better be necessary.

Jimmie pulled a pointer from his pocket and used it to pull back the tall reeds. Xander inched closer to peer over the plants. He looked down at Kais Bisset. His mangled body looked like it had spent the night in a meat grinder. With his hands and feet bound together, his distorted body formed an odd angle. From the swelling on his face, he'd taken a beating before someone put a bullet through his forehead.

Xander stepped backward and blinked. There was no way to erase Kais' tortured body from his memory. This was going to devastate Eliza and Luc. "What do you know, Jimmie?"

"This is your guy, right? The one that owns the storage unit. There is no ID on the body."

Xander nodded.

"The coroner is on the way. We suspect he's been here a few hours. Rigor mortis has started to set in. What do you know about this?"

"Eliza called me this morning. She was certain he was missing. He never went to bed last night and his car was still in the garage."

"And where was she last night?" Jimmie made notes on his phone.

"You don't think she did this, do you? Women don't shoot people in the head. I can tell you if she wanted him dead, she would have poisoned him or killed him while he was sleeping. This is too violent for her."

"I'm just asking questions right now. Where were you?"

Xander pointed his finger at Jimmie. "This is not the time for jokes. Has anyone told Eliza yet?"

"Negative."

Jimmie smacked him on the back. "You're the one with the unpleasant task of telling the family, Xander."

"Yeah," he agreed.

"We need to stem the pile of dead bodies. This doesn't help our tourism trade." Jimmie slipped his phone into his pocket. "I don't have the manpower to solve this chaos, so please find out who is disrupting our peaceful island." Jimmie walked back the way they'd come. Omar and Xander followed. Xander's steps were as heavy as the task facing him.

CHAPTER 13

Olivia walked the length of the living room. There used to be a time when she thought the view of the sky and the ocean could ease any angst. Realizing how wrong those simple thoughts were didn't sit well on her shoulders. Maybe giving Xander an ultimatum about the shooting range was a bad idea. In her head was the only place she'd admit it was a test. Would he, could he, ever put her in front of his work? In the beginning, she was certain she came first, but now she wasn't as adamant.

If he arrived home in the next ten minutes, making their appointment was still possible. She peered through the window to see Omar's car pull into the lane. Xander jumped out and raced up the stairs. She opened the door before he unlocked it.

"Just in time." She handed him the leather bag containing their guns and followed him to his car. She would have gone without him, but she didn't want to go alone. They were pulling in opposite directions. Xander's presence was so large, he could suck up all the air the moment he walked in a room. Could she marry him and not lose herself?

After two years, she should have found her place in his life, but she was still groping for her identity in his surroundings.

"I got the impression this wasn't the time to stand you up." He slid into the driver seat and started the engine.

She planted a kiss on his cheek. "Smart man. I would have gone without you."

"I know. I don't understand where this drive to become a precision shooter is coming from." He pulled out of their lane and headed toward the main road.

"I've been talking about going for months. This training will come in handy. It's better to have it and not need it than need it and not have it, right?"

He made a sound that was more of a snort than a chuckle.

"What does that mean?" she asked.

"Nothing."

He was probably thinking about her stalling on setting a date. Instead of pushing him to admit it, she kept quiet. A conversation about the wedding would put them in a foul mood.

At the range, she climbed out of the car before he reached her door. Once in the shooting stall, she unpacked the Glock. The gun was heavier than she remembered. She shifted it from one hand to the other until it felt comfortable, then she took her familiar stance. The one taught by her father.

Xander stood behind her. He widened her stance and leveled her arms. "How does that feel?"

"Not as comfortable as I was before, but maybe that's because it's different." She stared down the lane at the half black silhouette.

"Give it a try," he said before stepping back.

She fired off several rounds, pleased with how natural it felt. Everything she used to know came back. Xander pressed the button to retrieve the target. He examined her work, running his finger from one shot to the next as if he were connecting the dots.

"Not bad. You're better than I thought. There's no single kill shot here, but you would take someone down."

"That's good, right? I'm not sure I could kill someone, but if I stop them, then that's good."

He kissed her forehead. "Let's hope you never have to point a gun at anyone. Do you want to try again?"

She nodded and assumed the same stance.

"Try to keep your arms up. I think you lower it a little after every shot." He leveled her extended arms.

By the time they walked out, her shooting showed improvement. "A couple more visits to the range and you'll be a worthy opponent if anyone dares to test you."

She nudged his shoulder, happy to hear his words. "With the work you do, it's good for me to feel more comfortable."

He reached for her hand, squeezing it harder than normal.

"You've been quiet. Tell me what's bothering you. Was it bringing me to the range?"

He pulled her in closer as they made their way to the car. "Not at all. Every minute I spend with you is a gift." Before they climbed into the car, he released her from the big hug but held onto her arms. Something was wrong.

"What is it, Xander? Just tell me."

"Kais is dead." He blew air out of his mouth and lifted his chin.

If he weren't holding onto her, her knees would have weakened. "What happened? Why are you just telling me?" She'd only met him twice, but the news pulled her close to tears.

Xander looked away and opened the car door for her. He was hiding something. She climbed in the car and had to wait for him to walk around.

When he started the car, she cleared her throat and positioned her body to face him. "Tell me, Xander. Stop hiding things from me. How did he die?"

"Someone killed him. Sometime late last night or early this morning. Jimmie found his body on the east side beach."

"Does Eliza know yet?"

He nodded as his face darkened.

"You told her, didn't you? Instead of Jimmie, you did it, right?" What was it about Eliza that kept him dangling on a string? She might be the woman in his life, but Eliza still had a place in his heart. And Olivia didn't want to share him.

"I had to. I'm the owner of the company. He was my client. Luc is my godson."

She fought back jealousy. "It's related to the Calvin thing, isn't it? How is Luc?" Her voice hitched. Questions fired in her head. "That little boy lost his father. What...what..." She swallowed. "Have you lost other clients?" Fear mounted in her chest.

"Not like this."

She shook her head. "This is too real. I liked it better when I didn't know your clients... when they were nameless, faceless people you went off to help."

"Try to calm down, Bae." He placed a hand on her thigh.

"I'm trying, but this is too close to home. Are you in danger?"

"No, honey. There's nothing for you to worry about."

Olivia held her palm to her breast. If she pressed hard enough, maybe the ache would subside.

CHAPTER 14

Xander pulled into the lane in front of their home. Even with the air on in the truck, it was still warm. He needed to get out and walk off his concerns. This wasn't Olivia's concern, and he couldn't saddle her with his business problems or Eliza's worries. At least Olivia had agreed that sitting in a fancy restaurant and trying to pretend their life was normal wouldn't work tonight.

He carried the pizza box into the house and placed it on the kitchen counter. "I need to take a walk, Bae." He shoved his hands in his pockets and headed toward the door.

"Do you have to go now? I don't want to be alone." The forlorn look on her face cracked his heart. He was strong enough for them both, but he needed a moment to fill his well. The body count was growing, and everyone wanted him to fix this mess. He would, but the plan was coming together slower than he wanted.

He took Olivia's hands and led her to the sofa. No matter how crazy the world became, she always came first—her safety, her well-being. She sat in the curve of his arm, allowing him to rock her back and forth. "I'm going to find out who's doing this. You don't need to worry. I've always been here to protect you and I always will."

She held on to him. "Will it be like this all the time? Worrying about what's going to happen next or jumping whenever the phone rings because it might be bad news?"

"Bae, I don't know what to tell you. Sometimes my work is dangerous. Most of the time, it's not, but I won't lie to you about it." He tightened his hold on her. "You're protected."

She gave an unconvincing nod. "I'm not questioning you, but you can't talk me into feeling comfortable and safe. Nobody will be able to do that for me." She jabbed her index finger into her chest. "It's something I have to do for myself."

"I get it."

"I have something I want to ask you but promise to answer honestly and not get angry."

His stomach pulled. Statements like that never ended well no matter how pretty the smile or how gentle the voice. "What is it? You can ask me anything, any time."

She crossed her legs. "Were you and Eliza involved?"

He dropped his head back. They hadn't talked about their old relationships, which was a good thing. But it was stupid to think they never would. "Are we going to do this, Olivia?"

"I want to know. I don't care about the ones that don't live on the island or the ones that don't leave lipstick on your shirt or call you early in the morning. I only want to know about Eliza."

For a moment he said nothing. Breathing in and out was enough to manage. His mind searched for an answer that wouldn't rip away the peacefulness of their relationship. He swallowed. "Yes. It was a long time ago, and it's been over for years." He kept his voice level.

"Did you love her?"

"There was no love. We were using each other to get over broken hearts. It was an ugly time for me."

"After your break-up with Hope?"

"Yes."

"I understand." She nodded as if she was absorbing his answer. "I've been in the same place. But when I moved on, I ended those entanglements."

"There is nothing between us. Now, we're 'almost' friends."

She lifted her chin. "Okay. But, I have another question that's more important."

The worst had to be over, he exhaled. "One more question and then I get to drill you."

"About what?"

"Your old loves. I've never asked, but you've opened the gate, so now I can."

"Okay." She paused before asking her question, slowly enunciating each word. "Is Luc your son?"

"Luc? Kais and Eliza's son?" He shifted to get a better look at her face.

"Of course that Luc. Do you know another?"

"Why would you ask me that? What would make you ask me a question like that?" He put more space between them.

"From the first time I saw him, I wondered. You and that little boy are so close. He may have Eliza's hair, but he has your eyes, your features. Even some of your mannerisms are the same. Is it possible?" She stood. Her voice was gentle, but that didn't make the question easier to answer.

Of course, it was possible. He'd looked at that little boy so many times and wondered the same thing. When Luc was an infant, he'd even asked Eliza, and she'd sworn there was no possibility. He faced Olivia. "I've asked Eliza that question twice. Both times, she assured me he wasn't. She accused me of reaching for straws and threatened to not let me see him anymore if I didn't stop." He pinched the bridge of his nose. "So, I left it alone."

"What do you want to ask me?"

"I don't know who you dated before me and I don't care. I only said that because you opened the door."

"But I haven't asked you to have our wedding at the home of one of my boyfriends. And I'm certain I don't have any children in the world."

He held up his palms to her. "Bae, I can't have this conversation right now. I've lost a team member and a client. I'm not having a good week."

"Why didn't you ask Eliza for a paternity test if you thought it was a possibility?"

He dropped his head. "I don't know. I'm not sure I want to know. They are a family. Luc is happy, he loves Kais. If I'd asked, I'm sure she would have said no and cut off all my ties with Luc." He shook his head. "Maybe I didn't want the responsibility or maybe Eliza was convincing with her denial. Besides, Eliza and I had a fling, a child would bind us together in a way I didn't want."

"Xander, that doesn't make any sense. You can't pretend you don't have a child because it doesn't fit into your plan. It's almost as if I don't know you at all. The man I thought I knew owns up to all his responsibilities even if it doesn't fit his lifestyle."

"It's not like that, Olivia."

"Did you think I wouldn't notice the resemblance? How can you people walk around and ignore what might be right in front of your noses?"

"You don't know that he's mine. I don't know if he's mine. If I was certain, then I would have investigated further, demanded to know." He stood. His body knotted in ways it hadn't before. "I need to get out of the house and take a walk. That's if you're done with your cross-examination." He walked out of the house without waiting for her reply.

He sprinted down the hill. The full run taxed his lungs and by the time he reached the bottom, he was panting. He dropped his head and rested his hands on his knees. When his breathing slowed, he kicked off his shoes, stuck his phone inside one, and crossed the sand. Even though he wore jeans, a shirt, and his briefs, he waded into the surf and dived into a wave. The cool water against his warm flesh shocked his system. The clothes were a drag on his ability to swim, but the activity helped clear his mind. Sure, it had been lofty to think Olivia could live on the island and see Luc without asking questions. Every time he looked into that little boy's eyes, his heart tugged at what could be. Maybe that's why he wanted to marry and start his own family—have children where there was no doubt he was their father. A paternity test would have answered his questions, but it could also dash all his hopes.

When his arms grew tired, he circled back to shore. His wet clothes were even heavier, but his head was clearer. Swimming helped him develop a plan. Three people were dead, and he held the thread to each of their death. He had a mess that needed fixing and no matter how difficult, he needed to do it now. Starting with Olivia.

He picked up his shoes, took out his phone, and then slapped them together to displace the sand. He trudged up the hill, working out the conversation in his head. Just beyond his house, a black sedan was parked at the curb under the purple crepe myrtle. That car didn't belong on this street, not this time of day or this close to his home. He studied the vehicle, making out two occupants. Both were looking down. He couldn't make out their features because of the dark tint on the windows. Before he got close enough to question the driver, the car started and pulled away. He glanced down at the tag number, but there was no plate on the car.

He stopped in front of the house to dial Omar. "I got surveillance on my place. A black sedan, no tag. The car pulled away before I could ask questions. Olivia is already nervous, and I don't want to take any chances until we know what's going on. I want a twenty-four-hour guard on the house. Keep it low key. Olivia doesn't need to know."

"Anything else?"

"Tomorrow, we'll map out a plan. Let's start early."

Omar agreed and disconnected the call.

In the house, he removed his wet shirt, and then went to Olivia's studio. He walked in the room and sat in the chair by the door. She glanced over her shoulder at him. "Feeling better?"

"Sorta. You're right, Bae. Just like always."

She faced him with her camera still in her hand.

"I'll ask for the paternity test. I've been avoiding it, afraid of the consequences, but you're right. About everything."

She lifted her camera, focused the lens and snapped several pictures of him.

"What are you doing?"

"I need to capture the moment when you admitted you were wrong, and I was right." Her face broadened into a warm smile.

"Promise you won't leave me if you find out I'm a baby daddy."

CHAPTER 15

Olivia zoomed the camera lens in on Xander's eyes. For the first time there was vulnerability there she wanted to capture. "It's hard to admit when you're wrong, isn't it?" she said.

"Don't push it. I didn't say I was wrong, I said you were right. There is a difference."

Thinking of Eliza as the mother of Xander's first child numbed Olivia. She tried to ignore the disappointment. It didn't mean he cared any less for her or the children they planned to have one day. But it meant Eliza had a claim on him. It explained why Eliza was so familiar with Xander and why she didn't hesitate to reach out to him whenever she wanted. Blaming him for not dealing with this before meeting her was useless, there was no way to rewind the clock.

She came closer to Xander and snapped several more pictures of him from different angles. When he folded his arms across his chest, she put her camera down. "Are you hungry? The pizza is probably cold by now."

He pulled her forward until she stood between his legs.

"Whatever happens changes nothing between us. I adore you, Olivia, and we're going to have our family."

She rested her head on top of his. "I know, baby. Do you think Eliza will fight you on doing the test?"

"I'm not worried about her," he said with conviction in his voice. He'd taken a big enough step for one day. They'd have to work out the details after he sat and thought for a while with what was about to happen.

Xander pushed up her tank and smothered her nipple with his mouth. The warm feel of his mouth sent a bolt of excitement through her, making her believe their love could overcome any problem. Never had she imagined a relationship this big and beautiful would happen in her life. With his coaxing, she stepped out of her clothes, then returned to her place between his legs. He planted kisses on her breasts, chest, and shoulders. Each one slow and deliberate. Her body warmed to his touch. The reaction so intense, the sensation felt foreign.

She tried to unbutton his jeans, but the wet denim made it difficult. He stood to help her. After he stepped out of his clothes, he pulled her down on his lap. The heft of his shaft throbbed against her thigh, but he wasn't in a hurry. She massaged the length of his penis as they kissed. She took her time, treasuring the moment. Time stood still and all the disaster of the day faded for a moment. "Come on, baby," she begged him.

He picked her up and stretched her out on the tiled floor. Starting at her neck, he planted kisses at the base of her throat, slow and gentle. Then he trailed his warm tongue down one side of her chest, circling back up the other side. She grabbed a fist full of curls and tried to contain the pleasure pulsing through her veins. Xander knew every button to push to get her aroused. Tonight, he teased out pleasure in ways he hadn't before. He reached the intersection between her thighs and stroked her flesh. Without being able to reach his penis, all she could do was allow the ecstasy to consume her body. Maybe he was trying to say he was sorry, or he loved her, or both. If tonight was about purging his soul, then she was the vessel where everything he had to give would be deposited.

He slipped his tongue inside her, and she arched her back off the floor to meet him. The repetitive movement pushed her toward pleasure. The potent energy connecting them held her. She tightened her fingers in his hair as warmth pooled in her core. Her body buzzed with anticipation as if she was at the top of a cliff preparing to jump. The sensation mounted, like water slowly filling a well. The only part of her body she could control was the moaning that slipped from her lips. With another swirl of his tongue, he sent her over the edge and she free fell back into love with him forgetting all the questions that had dogged her for days. They'd find a way to work things out. Their life together was too beautiful to give up.

When she could place her hips back on the floor, she caught her breath. "Want to explain what that was about? Were you trying to excise pent up frustration?"

"The only thing that frustrates me is anything that keeps me away from you, that keeps us apart. If I can't spend every minute of every day with you, then something is wrong with the world."

"You always say the right thing at the right time." She climbed on top of him and kissed him with the same passion he'd shown her—slipping her tongue around his, demanding his full attention. She kissed his neck and gripped his penis. Each time she touched him, he moaned. His moans grew louder as she neared her target. Her goal was to do to him what he'd managed to do to her. She wouldn't come close, but the effort was the only thing that mattered. She circled her tongue around the tip of his shaft until his hips circled in rhythm with her. Moments like this, there was no room to question if they were destined to be together forever. Their connection was so tight, nothing could come between them. Not Eliza, not Luc, not his work, and not her insecurities. His body stiffened, and she knew she'd given him the same joy he'd bestowed on her.

She allowed him to catch his breath, then he stood and held out his hand.

"Part two happens in the bedroom," he said.

She accepted his hand and followed him through the house to the bedroom. "Let's bring the pizza."

"It's cold," he said, but he picked up the box and balanced it on his palm as they made their way to the bedroom. She climbed into bed before him and spread her legs.

"That's not fair." He put the pizza on the bench at the foot of the bed and climbed between her legs. "I might as well face it. I'm addicted to you," he sang.

"You are good at a lot of things, but singing isn't one." She held on to him so he couldn't move away. "But, baby, you can sing to me every night."

He kissed his way from her knees, along her thigh, then licked the entrance to her soul. Her body melted into the mattress when he climbed on top of her and slipped inside. His moves were slow. He pumped against her as if time stood still. Together, they could conquer anything that tried to come between them. She was sure.

Xander buried his face next to hers and their bodies moved in sync. It was a dance they'd done from their first time together and it only got better. She tightened her arms around him and made a mental note that what they had was worth fighting to keep. When his movement grew slower, she knew he was close to climaxing, but she couldn't wait for him. With her legs around his waist, she held on to him as her body pulsed with pleasure. Within seconds, Xander's body tensed as he caught up to her.

She continued to hold on to him long after her heartbeat and breathing returned to normal. "You know, I never thought it was possible to love someone so much. It's scary."

He rolled next to her. "You don't have to fear anything with me."

"Why? Can you promise you'll never break my heart, you won't get hurt, or die?" She placed her arm over his chest.

"Never on purpose." He gave her a tender kiss, the kind that was meant to seal his promise.

She was content to stare at the wooden beams in the ceiling until she remembered the car. "Did you see that black sedan parked down the street when you came back from the beach?"

He scrambled out of her arm and onto his knees, gesturing with his hands. "You saw that? Why didn't you say something?"

"Of course, I noticed it. The car was like a dead fish flopping on the beach. Nobody parks a car on top of the hill unless they're going down to the beach, but I never saw anyone get out." She came to her knees, too. "I took a few pictures with my telescopic lens."

Xander scurried off the bed. "You did what?" His voice was firm. Gone was the glow of their lovemaking.

"I took some pictures. What's the big deal?"

He paced at the foot of the bed. Olivia couldn't tell if he was upset or angry. The way he kept looking over at her and marching like a soldier, he could have been a bit of both.

"I don't understand why you're upset. I took a couple of pictures. What's the big deal?"

"You could have been hurt. You should have said something the minute I walked in the house. You should never take chances."

"I was minding my business. How is that taking a chance?"

"Anytime something seems odd, you need to tell me."

"What do you think I did, walk up to the car and take the pictures while the driver was looking at me?" She shook her head with such force her hair swayed. "I'm not stupid. I was inside the house. I took the pictures because I thought it was odd that the car sat there so long and no one got out."

Xander held up his hand, stopping her. "Bae, I'm glad you got the pictures. They might help me, but what you did was also dangerous. If something happened to—"

"You want to see the photos, don't you?" She grinned.

"Damn right I do." He reached for her hand and pulled her off the bed. "This could be the break Omar and I have been looking for. But I have to be careful giving you too much praise or you'll think you're ready for a permit to carry your gun in your purse."

Together, they made their way to her studio. She settled behind the desk. After connecting the camera to the computer, she scrolled through the photographs. She'd taken so many, she had to find the best ones. Xander pulled his chair so close she could hear him breathing as his hairy leg brushed against her.

She pointed at the screen. "These are the best ones. The tinted windows make it hard to see the finer details, but you can see two images. They're big guys. They weren't here for the surf since you can see they're dressed in light colored shirts."

"Two white men parked feet away from our house. Did they ever get out of the car?"

"Not while I was watching. I started to sneak off the balcony and up the hill to see if I could get a shot of the back of the car—capture the tag number."

He narrowed his eyes. "You wouldn't dare, would you?"

76

"No."

"Thank you." He pecked her lips. "There was no tag on the car."

She shrugged a shoulder. "I wasn't afraid, I knew you'd have a spasm if you found out." She held his face between her palms. "I did get a close up of the registration sticker in the window." She pointed. "See, I can make out the numbers. I'm sure if you give that info to Jaysa, she can track the car down, right?"

There was admiration in Xander's eyes as he gave his slow nod of approval. "Woman, every time I think I've figured out who you are and what you're capable of, you show me another side I didn't know you had. Now, I'm going to show you what I can do." He grabbed her by the waist. "Come with me and bring that scrap of paper." He pointed to the paper with the registration number penciled on it.

In his office, he turned on his computer. After several screens, he typed in the registration number she'd captured. "Omar and Jaysa aren't the only ones who can find and track information. I've got skills too."

He studied the screen for several minutes, and his shoulders sagged. "I knew it." He smacked the desk. "I damn well knew it."

"What? Knew what?"

"The pool hall owner, Ed. It's his car. When I asked him about a dark sedan, he gave me a snide remark as if... Well, at least now I know where to begin this investigation."

"You're not going to start tonight, are you? I mean we were getting ready to eat cold pizza and make wicked love all night long."

He studied her for a moment. She was certain he would pick up the phone from the way he tapped his index finger near the receiver.

"I dare you," she said.

"Okay, but first thing in the morning," he said, standing.

She draped her arms around his neck. "Let's celebrate this find with a bottle of wine and our cold pizza."

She led him to the kitchen. For the first time in months, there was satisfaction in her steps.

CHAPTER 16

Xander settled into the chair behind his desk. Every seat in his office was full this morning. Omar sat in his usual chair. Jaysa was at the table with her computer in front of her, the glare from the screen glowing on her face, and Olivia sat across from Jaysa.

Xander rubbed his hands together. "With all this brain power in my office, we'll come up with some answers today." He looked around the room. "Okay, who wants to go first?"

Jaysa raised her hand like someone seated in a classroom. Her computer knowledge was exceptional. Fresh out of college, Xander had to do a lot of talking to convince her to move back to Sebastian and work with him. In the end, he was sure her parents living on the island was the deciding factor even though she pretended it was the large salary he offered. She wore her hair short and tapered, which high-lighted her large brown eyes and full lips. Her complexion was the same rich brown as Olivia's. Jaysa tapped a few keys on her computer without looking up. "I found nothing on the customer list from Eliza that connected to anyone with the initials LC, but Bisset's customers have deep pockets. The money they spend on paintings is ridiculous. I was able to follow the last five transactions from beginning to end. They all checked out. I saw where the Bisset's purchased an expensive collection from a private seller in France for ten million dollars, but I don't see any transactions where they sold any of those pieces. How can they hold on to inventory that expensive? If the paintings weren't for them, why buy that many and hold them in a warehouse? It doesn't make sense."

"How many paintings are you talking about?" Omar asked.

"Three. But the information Eliza provided doesn't list the artist."

Xander rubbed his chin. "I don't know a lot about the art business, but is that unusual – an invoice without the name of the artist?"

"Very," Jaysa and Olivia said in unison.

"Unless the buyer requests anonymity," Jaysa added.

"Everything about the Bissets is unusual." Olivia's sarcasm didn't go unnoticed.

"Maybe they were going to start a gallery," Omar said.

"No," Xander shook his head. "Eliza didn't mention anything about a gallery nor did Kais."

Jaysa held up a finger. "There is one more thing. I've been able to track text messages and phone records—"

"Hacked is more like it," Omar grinned.

Jaysa rolled her eyes. "Anyway, there are a lot of text messages between Jeffrey and Eliza. They talked or texted several times a day. She didn't have that much contact with anyone else in the business. I think that's worth digging into and you can bet I will."

"That's why I hired you... your natural ability to be nosy." Xander chuckled.

"And that's why I took the job. I get paid to snoop around in other people's business." She stood and curtsied then returned to her chair. "I also tracked Kais' calls. There was a number for someone in New York that he talked with several times in the last few days."

"The night he went missing, who did he call?" asked Xander.

Jaysa studied her computer. "Let me see. You, the warehouse switchboard and a number I haven't run down yet."

"That checks out," Xander said.

"Why would she call Jeffrey so much? You mean to tell me the great Mrs. Eliza Bisset may have a dark secret?" Olivia looked across the room and locked eyes with Xander. He knew better than to bait her by commenting. She would never like Eliza.

"Well, there may be a good reason for all that contact. But I'll find out," Jaysa said.

Omar sat up straighter in his chair. "I'll ask around, too. If anyone ever saw the two of them together, somebody on the island can't wait to gossip about it."

"Okay, so far we know the car is registered to Ed. We need to find out how he's involved. We need to check out Eliza and Jeffrey to see what they had so much to talk about, and we need to find out who Kais called after talking to me and why."

"Good work on finding out about the car." Omar shifted his position.

"I can't take credit for this information." Xander nodded toward Olivia. She sat with her legs crossed showing off her bronzed glow as if she was posing for a photo shoot.

"Good work, Olivia. You have a little sleuth in you," Omar grinned across the desk at Xander.

Xander cleared his throat. "Okay, you two, can we focus on business? I think the bigger question is why are they watching my place?" He rubbed his chin. There was no time to shave this morning before the crew assembled, so there was plenty of stubble.

"Maybe they think you know something about the missing artwork," Omar said.

Xander nodded in agreement. "Omar, have the recordings from the pool hall yielded any useful information?"

"Recordings?" Olivia pushed to the edge of her seat.

Xander filled her in on the recording devices they placed in the pool hall.

"I wasn't expecting that answer, but I guess I should have," she mumbled.

"Expect us to do anything."

Her eyes registered surprise at Xander's comment. He turned to Omar. "Play what you've got so far."

Omar set the miniature device on the center of the desk and turned it on. "I'll fast forward through the bullshit and get to the good part." After a few starts and stops, Omar allowed the tape to play.

"What's going on?" A heavy voice said.

"We had some company yesterday. Showed a picture of one of my cars and asked about the drivers." Ed's voice was identifiable by his gruffness.

"Do you know who they were?"

"Never seen 'em before, but it was obvious they didn't belong in this part of the city."

"Does this look like one of them?"

"Yep, that's him. The one who did all the talking. What's his deal?" Ed said.

Xander looked across the desk at Olivia. Worry lines creased her forehead.

"He runs a security company. Nothing for you to worry about. If he becomes a problem, we'll take care of him."

Olivia gasped and covered her mouth.

"Stop the tape, Omar," Xander pointed to the device. "Bae, are you okay?"

She used her hands to signal she was okay. "I'm not used to hearing people talking about doing harm to someone else. When he said take care of you, he meant—"

"Bae, I'm a big boy. I'm used to that kind of talk."

"I'm not."

He stood. "Do you want to go to your studio while we finish up here?"

She shook her head. "No. No. I'm okay. If I'm lucky, I'll never get used to it."

"We're big boys. We do a good job of taking care of those that try to push us around," Xander assured her.

She looked from Xander to Omar before saying she was ready to restart the tape.

Omar resumed.

"I don't want no trouble and I don't want to know what you guys are into. All I want is you guys out of my life. You got it?"

"When we're done, we're done. And we ain't done yet. You ain't chicken, are you? I told you LC plays for keeps. You can't back out now."

There was some unidentified tussling on the tape before Ed continued. "I ain't indebted to anyone. I'm my own boss, and I'm too old to take orders from some faceless asshole I don't even know. When I say I'm out, I'm out."

The man with the heavy voice laughed. "Not anymore you're not. LC is going to use the car a few more days."

"Fuck, man. I'll give you another week, but that's it. You guys need to be more careful. That's why that white guy was in here. You got sloppy."

"You'll think of something to get him off your back. You're a big boy."

There was a long gap where nobody talked. Footsteps indicated someone walked away.

"Fucking idiots. They must think I'm some country boy they can fuck over." It was Ed's voice.

Omar stopped the tape. "Either Ed was talking to himself or someone across the room because that was the end of that conversation. The rest is normal business."

"We'll leave the devices in for a few more days and see if we can collect anything else." Xander pulled a pad from the drawer.

"Do you think that was the same guy parked across the street yesterday?" Olivia's voice quivered.

"I have no idea, but don't worry. We're on high alert. We've got safety systems in place." He faced Omar. "I think we can lean on Ed. He doesn't sound happy with the deal he's made, so maybe he'll be ready to turn on his handlers. Find out where Ed lives and let's follow him a bit. I'd like to catch him off guard. Check with other businesses in the area to see if any of them have security cameras. I want to know what these guys look like. There has to be facial photos of them somewhere."

"No problem," Omar said.

"Send someone down to the pool hall to hang around. I want someone on the inside," Xander said.

"How can you two be so cavalier?" Olivia's eyes were wide.

He and Omar exchanged glances. Her question wasn't what he expected. "This is what we do, Olivia. We're trained for this and we're prepared. Everyone sounds tough. They have to in order to exist in this arena."

She scooted to the front of her chair. "If I see the car outside again, I'll get a better picture. I was fooling around before. I didn't know how important it was."

"Don't go near the car, Olivia. I think these guys are murderers."

"I'm no idiot, Xander."

The phone rang. "It's Eliza," he said. His hand was poised above the receiver.

"Aren't you going to pick up?" Olivia drilled him with a stare.

"Eliza, what can I do for you?" He tried to sound casual. The daggers in Olivia's eyes were painful to watch.

"I need help. I need to go to New York to complete business."

"I don't understand what that has to do with me." He measured his voice to stay professional.

"It's Luc. I don't want to take him with me, and I was hoping he could stay with you and Olivia."

He glanced across the table at Olivia. "What about his nanny? Isn't that what nannies are for?" He put the phone on mute to tell Olivia about the request.

"Why, is something wrong?" Olivia wanted to say more, he could tell.

He shrugged a shoulder and turned off mute.

"The nanny flew out of here when she found out Kais was killed as if she thought the whole family was marked for murder." Eliza paused. "Luc's been through so much, Xander. He knows you. I don't want to leave him with a stranger... Please, I don't know who else to ask. I don't have family here and he has so much fun whenever he visits you guys."

"Let me talk to Olivia. I'll call you back." He hung up.

"I think that's my cue to get out of here." Omar gathered his stuff and hurried out.

"I'm with you." Jaysa grabbed her computer and followed him.

Olivia stood, pulling her hair back into a giant afro puff. "Your girlfriend wants us to babysit? For how long?"

"Just a few days. The nanny quit, and she doesn't have any other family on the island." He settled back in the chair. "This would be the perfect time to do the paternity test."

"Suppose Eliza fights you on this? Doesn't that concern you?"

"She doesn't have to know. I can get him swabbed while he's here."

"No, don't do it behind her back. Tell her you want to know." She came around the desk and leaned into him. "That's the only way we can do this. Tell her first. You've got a bargaining chip, use it." She pointed a finger at him. "Promise me."

He exhaled through his mouth and nodded. "You sure you're okay with this? Because of this case, the weight is going to fall on you for most of his care and you're not…"

"It's not a problem. Luc can hang out with me. I've got some calls to make about the wedding and I plan to play in the sand. I think I'll do more playing than planning."

"Maybe that ought to be the other way around."

She narrowed her eyes and walked out of his office.

CHAPTER 17

Xander scratched his head. There were several questions left open with the Bisset case, and the answers weren't coming easy. The paperwork Eliza had provided was spread out in front of him on the desk.

"You've been studying those papers for hours. Do you think what you're looking for is going to magically appear?" Omar asked without looking up from his phone.

"It's as if they ran two different businesses. Kais has stuff, Eliza has stuff, and nothing matches up." He looked up from the documents. "Kais told me the warehouse unit was empty. A decoy. So, what do you think was in those boxes we watched them unload from the unit and why would Kais lie to me?"

"Maybe he didn't know about the boxes. Did you ask Eliza if she knew what was in there?"

Xander scribbled a note. "I didn't, but I will." He pushed away from the desk. "Let's take a ride. I want to go through Kais' home office again. Maybe I overlooked something the first time. And I want to stop by and talk with Jimmie. The coroner should have the autopsy results on Kais."

Eliza opened the door after the third ring but blocked the entrance. "What are you two doing here? I wasn't expecting you."

Xander stepped forward. "I wanted to look through Kais' things again." He tried to sound relaxed, hoping she'd yield to his charm.

She looked at him and back at Omar before allowing them inside. "Can you make this quick? Luc will wake from his nap soon, and I don't want him to see you guys rummaging through his father's stuff."

"Sure." Xander motioned Omar to follow him. "Eliza, there were boxes at the warehouse that were stolen after the...the..."

"Go ahead and say it, Xander. The murders. That's what it was... Murder." She sounded hostile.

"I was trying to spare you," Xander said.

"Well, you can't." She spat out the words before coming to a stop outside Kais' office. "And before you ask, I don't know anything about that warehouse. The police already asked. If you want to look through Kais' desk, then do it, but don't interrogate me. I'm not answering anymore questions." She pinned Xander with a cold stare before walking away.

"If we thought she was going to be helpful, I think we better come up with another plan." Omar sat behind the desk and started opening drawers.

"I've been through his drawers. If something was there, I would have uncovered it by now. I was hoping we could have a conversation with Eliza, but she isn't cooperating."

Omar stood and glanced at the bookcase. "You're not surprised, are you?" He fingered the books before pulling out a slip of paper. "What's this?"

Xander stepped closer. "Hmmm, Renoir... and a name

and address for someone in California. Eliza doesn't know about this piece of paper." He slipped the paper into his pocket, "So she can't miss what she doesn't know about."

"Are you thinking the same thing I'm thinking?" Omar asked.

"The other buyer?" Xander nodded. "I'll have Jaysa check it out."

They made their way back to the car.

"Aren't you going to tell Eliza we're leaving?"

"She'll figure it out." Xander started the car and pulled away.

"Why do you think Eliza was so jumpy?" Xander asked Omar as they made their way up the stairs of the police building.

"Oh, she's hiding something. Are you sure she's not the one who killed her husband?"

Xander lifted an eyebrow. His instincts told him Eliza wasn't a killer, but he'd been wrong before. "If she did, she had to have help. She couldn't have killed him and hauled his body clear across town and up onto that dune alone."

"With those looks, that charm and all that money, she could convince almost anyone to help her."

Together, he and Omar walked into the police building. It was difficult to think of it as a department, there was only a handful of men and not a lot of technology. Jimmie's office door was open, so there was no need to knock.

"Why am I not surprised to see you two?" Jimmie pushed away from his desk. "Have a seat, gentlemen. Are you here to answer questions?"

"We're here to ask more than answer," Xander said.

Xander and Omar sat in front of Jimmie's desk. "We're following up to see if you have any information to share on the murder of Kais or the two men at the storage facility?" Xander asked.

Jimmie placed his hands on his protruding belly. "I've gotten a lot of calls. Sebastian is a small island. Three murders in two days makes for a lot of television coverage. Do you know how many international journalists have come here to ask questions? This case even made news in the States. Are you ready to tell me what you know? I need to play this investigation by the book. I've got everyone clamoring for details, even the prime minister wants information." Jimmie grabbed his pad and balanced it on his knee.

"I talked with Kais the night before he went missing. All he told me was that one of his clients threatened him. Someone he only knew as LC who lives in the States. It had something to do with a painting."

"That's it?"

Xander shrugged. "You don't want me to start making up shit to satisfy you, do you?"

"What's the possibility your client was into drugs?"

Xander looked to Omar.

"Nothing I've uncovered points to drugs. Why?"

"Both Jeffrey and Calvin had cocaine in their system," Jimmie said without breaking eye contact. "Trace amounts were also found in the fibers of their clothes."

"How about Kais?" Omar asked.

"He was clean, but they worked for him. Maybe he was the dealer." Jimmie pulled back to his desk and rested his elbows on the surface. "I have intel of a major drug group operating on the island. I think your guy was into more than fine art."

Xander shook his head. "I don't see Kais as that kind of man. He was too high brow for drugs. Isn't it possible he had nothing to do with the drugs? Maybe his man Jeffrey had a side hustle," Xander said.

"Along with your man, Calvin?"

"You think Calvin was selling drugs?" Omar raised his voice.

"I know you don't want to think anyone on your team is dirty, but we've been to his place. The information and paraphernalia we found are pretty hard to ignore." Jimmie tapped his pen on the pad in front of him.

Omar shifted in his chair. His face was taut. "I can't believe that. Can we look through the stuff you collected?"

Jimmie scratched his chin. "It's evidence. I'll let you take a glance at what we've collected, but nothing leaves the building."

"Sure." Xander stood. "We both want to find out who's behind these killings. But I agree with Omar, something isn't adding up."

Jimmie shrugged. "The evidence is what the evidence is." He led them down the hall and into a room filled with conference tables. Each one was cluttered with a variety of personal items. "The evidence from Calvin's place is on the table to the right. Jeffrey's things are on the table to the left. Someone is coming in soon to tag and bag everything."

From a box just outside the door, Jimmie pulled two pairs of latex gloves and held them out. "Take pictures, but don't touch anything. Like I said, everything about this case is by the book. I don't want anyone else looking over my shoulder."

Xander extracted his phone from his pocket, then turned to Omar. "I'll photograph Calvin's stuff, you get Jeffrey's."

Jimmie rested against the doorjamb, while Xander and Omar snapped pictures.

Xander finished and returned to the doorway. "You'll keep me posted if you find out anything. Won't you, Jimmie?"

"The bigger question is will you keep me informed? You always find a back door with all the answers."

Outside the police building, Xander climbed into the driver's seat.

"Do you believe Calvin was dirty?" Omar asked.

Xander folded his lips together. "I'm going to withhold judgment. We don't have enough information yet. But if he had cocaine in his system, he violated our number one rule, didn't he?" Xander checked his mirrors and pulled into traffic. "When you talked to the family, did you get any indication from them that he might have been into illegal activity?"

"None. I told them he was dead. They cried. I wasn't there to interrogate them." Omar's hostile tone didn't surprise Xander. Omar was loyal and expected the same in return.

"I'm not questioning your tactic with the family. You did the right thing." He made a sharp right turn. "Maybe it's time for another visit."

"That family is in mourning. We can't ask his mother if her son was a drug dealer."

Xander gave his assistant a sharp look. "I have no intention of tormenting Calvin's grieving mother. But if Calvin isn't into drugs, I want to clear his name. Where does she live?"

After providing the address, Omar remained quiet for the rest of the ride.

When Xander stopped in front of the small home of Calvin's mother, he turned off the car. "Are you coming in?"

"This doesn't feel right."

"Stop worrying. I know how to be tactful, Omar. Trust me," Xander said.

The two of them frequently disagreed on the right approach. Omar had a hard edge that wasn't often touched by the tender side of life.

"You've got to trust me." Xander opened the car door and stepped out, leaving Omar to make his decision.

He'd rung the bell before Omar walked up behind him on

the porch. They exchanged glances, then Xander slapped him on the back.

A woman that had to be Calvin's mother opened the door and peered through the screen. Her hair was salt and pepper, but it had the same curly texture as Calvin's. She was much shorter than him, but there was no mistaking that the spacing between their identical brown eyes was the same.

"Please come in." She opened the screen door. "The family is gathering in a few hours at the funeral home. We need to make final arrangements for Calvin. I still can't believe my precious baby is not coming over for Sunday dinner. He loved my paella." The longing in her eyes as they filled with tears was too much to observe. Xander took the older woman in his arms and held her.

"If there is anything you need…"

"You've done so much already. We'll be fine." She patted his back before breaking the embrace to pull a tissue from her dress pocket, and then dabbing at her eyes.

"I'm going to find out who did this. It's our number one case right now." He still held her by the shoulders. "Can we talk to you for a moment before you leave?"

"Yes, sure." She pointed to the sofa. "I'll tell you anything you want to know."

"Can you give us a list of his closest friends?" Xander asked.

She ran off several names, which Omar wrote in his pad. "Calvin used to hang with a bad bunch, but working for you was good for him. He loved the job. He was always talking about how he was going to make you proud."

When it was clear she had nothing else to share, Xander stood. "We should let you and the family finish your business." He pretended to step toward the door. "Did Calvin have any items here?"

"His bedroom looks the way it always did. Sometimes after Sunday dinner, he'd stay over. You know—"

"Yes, we know he loved your cooking. And we all love your banana cream pies." Omar spoke for the first time since entering the house.

She gave them a weak smile. It didn't stay on her face long. "His bedroom is down the hall on the left. His brother and sister are here." She patted Xander's arm. "I trust you, lock up on your way out." She picked up her purse and walked out the door.

Calvin's childhood bedroom looked exactly the way Xander imagined. His varsity trophies lined the dresser and posters of two female hip-hop groups were pinned to the wall.

Omar opened the drawer to the table closest to the bed and flipped through some papers. "What do you make of this?" he asked.

Xander took the papers from Omar. Several handwritten phone numbers were in the right-hand corner of the page. An address in New York and three others on the island. Jeffrey's name was scratched in bold black letters and the name Lawrence Cistos. "I think we've come across our second crack in the case."

CHAPTER 18

Sitting in on Xander's meeting wasn't the smartest idea Olivia ever had. In those few hours, she'd learned enough to scare her even more. Maybe Xander's occupation was more dangerous than being a police officer. She shuttered. But they weren't on a television show or in a movie. This was real life and bad things happened. Look at what happened to Kais. One day he was throwing a party, the next day he was dead.

On Thursday afternoon, Olivia made her way to Old Towne. Since moving to the island, she'd made fast friends with Adisa, the owner of Sebastian Treasures, the best art and gift store on the island. Today was the second time she'd done promotional photos for the shop. Adisa liked putting out a new brochure every few months. Small jobs like this didn't pay much money, but the cost of living on Sebastian didn't require the same amount of income as living in New York. Plus, the customers on the island weren't as critical as fashion magazines or hotel chains.

Olivia was greeted by Adisa as soon as she walked in the shop. Olivia's assistant, Miles already had the lights set up and was busy arranging the sculptures on display. Working without Gwen took some getting used to, but at least she'd found someone to handle the heavy equipment and the lights. Unlike Ajay, her previous assistant, Miles was old enough to be her father and married to the love of his life. He treated her like a daughter, and the thorough background check Xander did on Miles to make sure he'd never stalked a woman was helpful, too.

"Don't you look like sunshine and happiness this morning." Adisa's heavy accent welcomed her.

"You know yellow is my favorite color." Olivia grabbed the hem of her flared skirt and fanned the pleats.

"And I can see why, it makes your skin glow." Adisa studied her for a moment. "We've talked several times about your work. Have you given any thought to when you're going to let me display your photographs?"

"Of course. And every time I do, I get nervous. I'll let you know when I'm ready. The offer doesn't expire, does it?"

"Of course not, my friend. Miles, talk her into it, why don't cha'?" Adisa spun around.

"I've tried," Miles said.

Adisa pivoted on her toes. "If you need me, I'll be in the back."

Olivia greeted Miles and removed her cameras from the bag. "We should be done here in less than an hour, Miles."

"Good. I'm taking the grandchildren to the beach today. We go every day." He chuckled. "But they're only here for a few weeks, and I want to spend as much time with them as I can."

"Maybe I'll bring Luc over tomorrow and we can join you and your bunch."

Miles gave her a wide smile. "The more the merrier. Besides, my wife and I could use an extra pair of hands. Those kids wear us out."

She took several practice photographs before examining them. The coloring was off. "Miles, can you adjust the lights? I'm picking up glare on the small mask."

He nodded and jumped to his feet to make the change. For a man his age, his flexibility was phenomenal even though he moved slow. Together, they breezed through the hour.

After the photo shoot, Miles fingered an authentic wood carving of a mother and son. "You know, Alberta and I are celebrating our forty-fifth wedding anniversary. That's why the grandkids are visiting. I was thinking about getting her something fancier this year." He held up the piece. "What do you think of something like this?"

Olivia pulled the camera strap onto her shoulder. "It's very nice. Do you know the artist is from Benin? My great-grandparents were from there. I've been studying the country."

"Chile, I wouldn't know the difference. It could have been made in China for all I know. But I think she'd like it." He examined the price stamped on the bottom of the piece. "Whew, lord. This is more expensive than I thought. This little thing costs three-hundred dollars."

She couldn't hold back her laughter. "Sebastian Treasures is more like a gallery than a souvenir shop. The pieces are exquisite. Besides, you don't want to give Alberta something cheap to mark that many years of marriage. She deserves a special piece." Olivia couldn't help but wonder if one day she and Xander would have that many years to celebrate. In his line of work, that was questionable.

Miles made a noise in his throat. "Yeah, and I just might leave the price tag on it so she'll know how much I spent on her."

She patted him on the back.

Adisa waved her to the back of the shop. "Olivia, I've got

some new pieces in the vault that just came in. I'd like to get some pictures of them to put on the website. I don't need them to be fancy." Whenever Adisa found an interesting piece of art, she called Olivia to take pictures. "You're the photographer, I'll show you the pieces I like, and you can use your judgment to group them any way you want."

Olivia followed her into the vault. Adisa lifted the heavy drape covering several canvas paintings. With her camera still on her shoulder, Olivia walked the length of the room examining the pieces, nodding at the beauty of the collection. "Are these originals or copies?"

Adisa drew back and eyed Olivia. "Girl, you know I don't sell junk," she said in her thick island accent. "If it's in my shop, it's authentic. You know that."

"I know, but this stuff is nice. Why haven't you put these pieces in the shop yet?"

"Some of them haven't been here long enough to catalog yet. Others, I think I can make more from private sales." Adisa fingered through the canvases, pulling out a few for special attention.

"Let me look through and pick out a few. I won't get everything in the brochure, but some of these will be incorporated for sure." Olivia snapped several pictures. This was the best part of her job, taking photos for fun.

"Why are these still covered?" She pointed to another grouping of pictures on the opposite side of the room.

"Those don't belong to the shop. I'm holding them for a customer."

"Mind if I take a peek?"

"No problem but be careful. I don't own them, so don't include those pieces in the pictures." Adisa uncovered the art.

Olivia got down on one knee to get a closer look. "These look like Renoirs."

Adisa scratched her head. "Like I said, I'm holding them

for a customer because I have the vault. He didn't ask me to authenticate them. My first guess says they're copies and not very good ones." She shrugged.

Olivia adjusted her lens and snapped several pictures of each piece.

"I don't want those pictures," Adisa said.

"I know. I just think they're gorgeous. I wonder if the owner would be interested in selling one. Maybe I could afford one. Can you tell me who the customer is?"

Adisa sucked her tongue. "Sure, Kais Bisset. You must know him. Everyone on the island knows the Bisset family."

Olivia stood and faced Adisa. "I know Kais and Eliza. You know someone killed Kais a few days ago?"

"I do. It's such a shame. He was a nice man. I called his wife to ask her what she wanted to do with the paintings. She hasn't decided yet, so I told her I'd hold them a few more days. That is one strange woman."

"Strange how?"

"Well, when I called her, she didn't know anything about them, but then she became agitated. I told her if the sale fell through, I could try to find buyers for her. I mean they're decent enough that someone might want to hang one in their home or office. I know the Bissets are rich; I'm quite surprised they're dealing in dime store art. And why he wanted me to place them in the vault is beyond me, but they can't stay in my place for too long. I'm not sure my insurance covers items that aren't purchased by the shop. So, she has to move them soon."

Olivia placed her hand on Adisa's shoulder. "Do me a favor. Don't tell anyone you have this collection, I mean no one. Promise me."

She shook her head. "Okay, but why?"

Olivia glanced at her watch. "I've got to run, but please

don't. As your friend, trust me on this." After Adisa agreed, Olivia gathered her equipment and rushed out.

When she walked through the door of her house, Olivia went to Xander's office without depositing her equipment in her studio. She allowed the camera bag to dangle from her hand, her shoulders were too tired to handle the weight. "I should have known the two of you would be in here with your heads buried in the computer and paperwork," she said to Xander and Omar. She rounded Xander's desk to kiss him.

"How was your photo shoot?" Xander pulled her down on his lap and pressed his lips against hers.

"Guess what I found?"

CHAPTER 19

Xander slipped his arms around Olivia's waist and listened while she told him about the art. When she finished, she looked at him, waiting on his approval. "You're serious, Bae?"

"Of course, I am. You know I couldn't make this stuff up. What are the chances?" Her hands were as animated as her voice.

"And Eliza knows the art is there? When I talked to her, she said she had no idea." Xander shifted and Olivia climbed off his lap and took the chair across from the desk. He wanted to pull her back, but he needed to focus on the info she'd provided.

"Adisa didn't say when she called Eliza, but Kais has only been dead two days. It had to be yesterday." Olivia leveled her gaze on him.

Eliza was never a forthright person. It was easier for her to tell a lie than to tell the truth. That was only one of the obstacles that blocked their relationship. And it seemed nothing had changed. "Why wouldn't she call me if she had information? Doesn't she want to help find the person who murdered her husband?" Xander pushed away from the desk and stood. "I'm supposed to pick up Luc today, so I'll have a chance to find out what she knows and what she's keeping from me. Olivia, call your friend at the art store and ask her to let you know if and when Eliza moves the painting. Omar, please check on our guys. I want to know if they have any information from the pool hall."

Omar nodded, and Xander watched the way his friend slogged toward the door. Calvin's death must have still had a grip on him. Knowing Omar, he wasn't going to shake it until he proved Calvin wasn't dirty.

Olivia uncrossed her legs and stood. "Whatever you do, don't make Eliza mad or she might not agree to the paternity test."

"I know how to handle Eliza." The answer was curt. To soften the moment, he pulled her into his arms. "I'm sorry, Bae, I didn't mean to take out my frustration on you." He kissed the tender slope of her forehead. No matter what was going on, she was the best part of his day. "I don't like being lied to. I knew she was keeping something from me, but I'll find out what's going on. And don't worry, I'll get the test."

Two hours later, Xander sat in front of Eliza's house, tapping his fingers against the steering wheel. Eliza was cunning. Her secrets were piling up like the dead bodies. He exhaled through his mouth. He needed to get answers about the paternity of Luc without turning her against him. If Luc was his son, Xander wanted to provide him the stability that Eliza alone couldn't now that Kais was dead.

Ignoring what was in plain sight had been too easy for four years. Luc was in a home with people who loved him and catered to him every minute. After Xander got the results, whatever they provided, nothing would be the same. Finding out the truth was unnerving enough to glue him to the driver's seat. Life was good, near perfect and upending everything could cause a disruption that might make recovery impossible.

Of course, Eliza would put up a fight. Luc was the only thing she cared about. She had cried when he told her Kais was dead, but it was a kind, polite sobbing like she was trying to remain strong. But asking her to share Luc, he expected worse.

He spotted Eliza coming toward him from the house. With a heavy breath, he stepped out of the car. Humidity hung over the island like a blanket. His shirt clung to his back, holding in the moist heat. "Eliza," he said, "how are you holding up?"

"I'm not. I'm faking it every day." She looked impeccable, not at all like a woman who was about to bury her husband. He gave her a warm embrace and couldn't help thinking about what Olivia would say about his familiarity with her. It pained him to think of hurting Olivia.

"I'm so glad you and Olivia agreed to look after Luc. While I'm in the States, I'll be so busy he might feel ignored. At a time like this, he needs as much attention as he can get." She waved her hand for him to follow her into the house.

As soon as they were inside, Luc bounded down the spiraling staircase and into his arms. "I'mma stay with you," Luc said in his high-pitched sing-songy voice.

"Yes, I know." Xander tickled Luc's neck with his nose. "We'll have fun."

"Have you decided which toys you're going to take?" Eliza poked her son in the side.

Luc stopped giggling and gave his mother his full attention. "Not yet."

"Then you must hurry. Mommy's got a lot of things to do and Xander is ready to take you."

Xander put Luc down and the little boy charged toward the stairs. "Can I bring my stuffed giraffe?" He asked Xander with the seriousness of an adult. Xander had bought the stuffed toy for Luc during his last trip to visit his parents.

"You can bring anything you want," Xander said. When the boy disappeared, he directed his attention back to Eliza. "I need to talk to you."

She stared at him for a moment before exhaling through her mouth. "Come on in my office, but I'm not sure I want to hear what you have to say. You've been full of nothing but bad news lately."

She closed the door but didn't offer him a seat. "Is this about Kais? Have you or the police found out who killed him? They asked me a million questions, but I'm not sure why. I don't know anything. For a moment, I believed they thought I had something to do with his death."

Xander nodded. It wasn't such a farfetched idea. "Any luck finding that painting Kais was working on for his client?"

She shook her head while looking at the stack of papers on her desk. One of Eliza's major faults was she thought she could outsmart everyone else. Her obvious lie was hard to witness.

"Are you sure you've told me everything? I mean it might be something small, but it could lead me to Kais' killer."

"I've told you everything I know." She continued to avoid looking at him.

"How about Jeffrey, the guy who worked for Kais, anything you can share about him?"

"What do you mean?" She fidgeted with her wedding rings, spinning them around her finger.

"How long did he work for you guys? Before he started checking on the storage unit, what were his duties? Did he get along with Kais? Did Kais trust him? Did you?"

She pinned him with a cold stare. "He was like...like Kais' right-hand man. You know, doing whatever Kais needed.

Escorting property from place to place. Couriering sensitive documents, that kind of thing. I had no contact with him, so I can't tell you much. Why is this important? And every time you see me, does it mean I need to be prepared to answer questions? You're more interested in investigating this case than you are with me and Luc."

"Like I said, the more I know, the faster we know what's going on." He shifted his weight. "Did you have any interaction with Jeffrey?"

She smacked her palm on the desk. "Why are you so interested in Jeffrey? Find out who killed Kais. He died before Kais, so he didn't do it." She sounded exasperated.

"Calm down, Eliza. I'm working on it. Don't you believe the murders are connected?"

"I don't know what I believe." She rubbed her forehead. "Look, I need to finish up some things before I fly to New York." She started toward the door.

He touched her arm. "There is one more thing, Eliza."

"What the fuck is it now, Xander?" Arms glued to her sides, her body was stiff.

"It's not about Kais. I want to talk about Luc."

Her face tightened, but her shoulders sagged enough for him to notice.

"Is he my son?"

Her eyes narrowed. "Why are you asking me that question now? Don't I have enough things to worry about? We've had this conversation more than once. I'm not in the mood to entertain your curiosity again." She turned her back to him and grabbed a tissue. With care, she dabbed under her eyes.

"I asked you the moment I found out you were pregnant. You said absolutely not." He dropped his head to get a better look at her face. "I remember that day. You were adamant. I've always wondered, Eliza. The timing..."

"I don't want to discuss this with you. He's Kais' son. He thinks Kais is his father. That's the only thing that matters."

He reached out and placed his hand on her arm. "I'm not trying to erase anything from your family history. I want to know. I deserve to know. I have a right to know."

"Why now, Xander?" She folded at the waist as if she'd been hit by pain and settled into the chair closest to her.

"Why not? Kais is gone, so you don't need to lie."

They stared at each other for several seconds, neither of them speaking. The room was charged with nervous energy. Eliza wrung her hands but didn't break eye contact with him. Their history told him she was ready for battle.

"I want you to know that while Olivia and I are watching him, I plan to do a paternity test."

"Suppose I tell you I don't want you to do that?"

"I'll ignore you." He sat and pushed his back against the chair. "I want to know, and nothing is going to stop me this time."

She shook her index finger at him. "You had this all planned, didn't you? That's why you jumped at the chance to watch him. Now I have no choice, not enough time to make other arrangements."

"Is he my son?"

"I don't know." She stood. "Of course, there is a chance he could be. But we had broken up when I found out I was pregnant, and Kais and I were dating. It was easier to let Kais think I was pregnant with his child."

Xander ran his hand over his face. "And what about me, Eliza?"

"What about you, Xander? You did everything you could to get far away from me. Kais was excited about the baby, so I decided to leave things alone."

He stood. "I want to know, and I won't let you push me off anymore."

She pointed her index finger at him. "If you and Olivia think you can take him away from me, I'll fight you to hell and back."

"We have no intention of trying to take him away from you. I only want to spend time with him."

"You won't say anything to Luc about this, will you? Tell him you're playing some kind of game when you swab his cheek, but don't you dare tell him why. If it turns out you're his father, then we'll tell him together. He's going through enough. I don't want my son traumatized."

"I adore Luc. He's my godson. I would never do anything to upset him, and you know that."

"What will you do if you find out that you're his father?"

"I don't know. I never wanted to think that far ahead. I've been reluctant to want so much."

"If you knew back when I was pregnant, would you have stayed with me? Would we have given our relationship a real chance?"

He didn't want to be angry with Eliza. He was just as guilty for not doing a paternity test sooner. There was no explanation for why he didn't. "I don't know. We don't know. Speculating now doesn't benefit either of us."

CHAPTER 20

Xander and Luc walked into the kitchen hand-in-hand. Luc had only been there one night, but the little replica of Xander had adopted Xander's morning expression of seriousness until after breakfast. If the two of them weren't blood-related, then Olivia would have to visit an ophthalmologist.

"What's for breakfast?" Luc broke away from Xander and charged toward her, grabbing her around the legs. She could almost pretend they were a family.

"I made your favorite, buttermilk pancakes with smiley faces." Olivia set the plate on the table in front of him.

"Let me help you with the syrup, Luc." Xander reached for the bottle.

"No. I do it." Luc demanded. He squeezed half a cup of the sugary sweetness on two small pancakes, and then pierced one with his fork.

"Are you sure you're okay caring for him alone today? With all that sugar, he'll be charged with extra energy." Xander removed the bottle of syrup from Luc's hand and set it on the opposite side of the table.

"I'm meeting Miles at the beach. He has his grandkids, so Luc will get to play with kids his age all morning." She walked to the far end of the kitchen and motioned for Xander to follow. "He's no problem. How about you? Did you get the sample?"

He patted his shirt pocket. "I'll drop it off before meeting with Omar. I've told them I'll pay extra for them to rush the results. Now that I know it's a possibility, I don't want to wait for an answer." He bit off a mouthful of bacon. "I promise to work from home the rest of the week to take care of Luc, so it won't all be on you."

She leaned in closer. "I got a call from Adisa this morning. Eliza called last night about the painting. She stopped by before Adisa closed and picked it up. Adisa said she was in a hurry and only wanted to take one of them. The larger one."

"She's probably halfway to New York already. Did Adisa say anything else?"

Olivia shook her head. "What do you think this means?"

"Eliza is lying about a whole bunch of stuff, and I can't trust her."

She wrapped her arms around Xander's neck and kissed his cheek. He smelled like soap and fresh air. Inhaling his scent, she ran her tongue along the column of his neck. He'd always spoken so highly of Eliza, admitting he couldn't trust Eliza took a lot for him. It had to be hard for him to see her in this light.

Olivia walked behind Xander as he made his way back across the kitchen and took the seat next to Luc. She tried to sound chipper. "Luc and I get to spend the day at the beach taking pictures of children playing in the surf. I got the better end of this deal."

"Luc, promise you'll be good for Olivia. She's the boss."

He nodded without looking up from his plate.

Xander kissed her, then tossed Luc's curls. "I should be back home for an early dinner."

By the time she and Luc arrived across town at Miles' house, they were an hour late. His wife, Alberta opened the door. "I know we're late, but I had no idea how long it would take to get me and a four-year-old out of the house."

"No worry, Chile. Miles and the kids just walked down to the beach. We're not as good at handling little ones as we used to be either. It's old age." She laughed, then pointed through the patio doors. "Leave your bag here and head on down. I'll be there as soon as I clear the morning dishes."

Luc yanked her toward the door. "Let's go." He dashed out the door ahead of her.

"Luc, you have to stay with me. Remember, I'm the boss today."

Olivia stepped through the door. It was getting hotter by the minute, but the ocean breeze made it feel a few degrees cooler. Miles waved her over as Luc slipped off his sandals and raced toward the other kids playing in the sand on the water's edge.

Olivia settled on the blanket next to Miles and exhaled through her mouth. "Whew. How can you handle that many kids for two weeks? I'm struggling with one."

Miles laughed. "Rules. Lots of rules." He stretched his legs out in front of him. "Do you ever leave home without your camera?"

"Seldom. I never know when I'll get a good shot. Plus, I might do a showing at Adisa's shop one day, so the more pictures I take, the more I'll have to choose from." She removed her camera from the bag and snapped on the lens. After focusing the camera, she took several pictures of kids building sandcastles. Miles lived on a public beach and it was crowded today. "I see several families had the same idea today." She used her chin to point at the masses enjoying the beach, and then started snapping pictures, trying to focus on the colorful towels, bright sun umbrellas, sand pails and beachballs flying in all directions. Getting releases from strangers might be an issue.

"Kids, come back this way. You're going out too far." Miles waved the children back toward the shore.

"Maybe I need to put Luc in his floaties." Olivia pulled them from the bag along with the sunscreen, kicking up sand as she made her way to the water's edge. She waved Luc over. "Let's put these on you."

"Do I have to? None of the other kids have them. I'm not a baby." He pouted.

Olivia got down on her knees. "How about you do it for me? I want to make sure you are safe and can have fun." She pointed down the beach. "See those kids? They have floaties. You'll be cool just like them."

He turned to stare. After a long moment, he held out his arms. She pushed the floaties into place and kissed his cheeks. "Now, I need to put more lotion on you, so you don't get a sunburn."

He shoved his foot in the sand and huffed. "I'm not a baby," he said again, but allowed her to slather on the cream.

When she finished, she said, "I'll have to make sure I tell your mom how good you've been."

He nodded before running back to the other children.

Alberta showed up with a basket of tuna fish sandwiches, potato chips, and little juice boxes with the straw glued to the side. The kids stopped long enough to eat half a sandwich and spill most of their juice. After helping Alberta clean up the mess, Olivia leaned toward Miles. "Should we keep them out of the water for an hour or so? You know that thing about swimming right after you eat?"

"I don't think they ate enough to count and what they're

doing isn't swimming," he laughed. "You are such a worry wart. Calm down. The kids will be fine."

She shrugged. "You know how it is when someone is in your care. I can't help worrying."

"Don't listen to him," Alberta chuckled. "He only half sleeps the whole time the grands are here just in case they have a bad dream or need us during the night."

Alberta mimicked Miles stumbling around with one eye opened. Olivia held her stomach and laughed.

"At least I know I'm not odd." Olivia grabbed her camera and jumped up. "The two of you squeeze in tighter. I want to take your picture. Miles, put your arm around Alberta and give her that goo-goo-eyed look."

He did as she asked. The two of them could have been her parents. The love they shared was visible in every snapped shot. A photo collage displaying their love would make an awesome anniversary gift.

Yelling behind her made her spin around. Miles' grandchild, Jason, was too far out in the ocean and drifting further. He flapped his arms as the water pulled him under. He popped up again, further from shore. Miles and Alberta scrambled to their feet. "Oh my God," Miles muttered as he ambled toward the water's edge, his age evident in every step.

Olivia dropped her camera, snatched off her sarong and charged into the water. By the time Miles reached Jason, it would be too late. The warm water engulfed her. When she was out far enough, she dived into the surf. The yells from the shore disappeared in the gurgling of the water as it rushed against her ears. The only thing that mattered was getting to Jason before he disappeared or was pulled too far away. Her arms sliced through the ocean like blades through bread. Within seconds, her arms started to burn. Xander could have done this without breathing hard. She wasn't sure she could make it to Jason and back without requiring help herself. Instead of thinking about the pain, she focused on reaching the boy. She came up for air within feet of him and pushed her body forward, ignoring the warning signs from her lungs.

As she reached for Jason, he continued to flail, slapping her around the head and shoulders. She outweighed him by at least sixty pounds, but she struggled to control him. "I've got you, Jason. Calm down," she urged while treading water. He took several breaths without swallowing water, and his body relaxed enough for her to control him.

She had to swim parallel to the shore until the current released them both. Her body ached like she was doing an intense two-hour aerobics class, but she forced her body to do what her mind willed it. About fifty yards further down the beach, she carried Jason to shore. Miles and Alberta waded into the water, and Miles eased his grandson from her arms. She rested her hands on her knees to catch her breath and alleviate the tightness in her triceps.

"Olivia, thank you so much." Miles gushed.

She nodded, still catching her breath, too exhausted to talk.

"Jason, how many times did we tell you not to go out that far?" Alberta admonished her grandson. His wide-eyed stare said he was too afraid to talk. He held on to his grandmother's neck like it was the anchor he needed. The crowd parted as they made their way back to their blankets. A few of the spectators clapped. Olivia bowed her head before scanning the children playing in the sand to catch a glimpse of Luc. He wasn't on the edge of the water with the other children that were oblivious to all the commotion. She spun around and checked the blanket. Maybe he wanted another sandwich.

"Where's Luc?" her voice wobbled. She spun around again, taking in the scene slower this time. He had to be here.

She searched for his bright orange floaties with blue whales. "Where's Luc," she yelled as she ran to the water's edge, searching the crowd then the surf. She pivoted on her toes, trying to see over the crowd. She shielded her eyes and checked the waves. "I don't see him. Luc," she called. "Luc. Luc. Luc." Each time she said his name, her voice grew louder and more panicked. She pressed her palm to her chest to keep her heart from jumping out. Miles and Alberta picked through the crowd calling his name too. The fear that overtook her was like poison coursing through her veins. The sickening feeling started slow but as each second ticked by, the overpowering clammy reality made it harder for her to move through the sand. It might as well have been quicksand.

Miles called his grandchildren. His face was as tight as Olivia's chest. She saw the fear in his eyes before he spoke to the gathered children. "Do you know where Luc is?" he asked his grandkids.

"He went with that man, his father."

"What man?" Olivia asked with so much force, the kids jumped. There was no man that could have rightfully taken Luc. His father was dead, and Xander wouldn't show up to take him without letting her know.

"I don't know. They went that way." One of the kids pointed to the path leading away from the beach.

CHAPTER 21

Xander found an empty parking slot in front of Omar's apartment. He dialed his number. "I'm outside."

"I'll be down. Give me a moment to gather some notes. I've got some interesting info to share."

Within minutes, Omar appeared at the door and started across the paved lot. In his hand, he held his infamous note pad. Omar was taller and heavier than Xander. If he was the muscle of the company, then Xander was the brain. They argued about their roles, which swapped depending on the circumstances. Xander rubbed his chin. To find out why Eliza was lying, he'd have to be a little bit of both.

Omar climbed into the car. "What's on the agenda today?"

"Eliza picked up the painting this morning. The one she told me she knew nothing about yesterday."

"You're surprised?" Omar lifted his eyebrows. "Did she also say she knew Jeffrey?"

"She rolled her shoulders and said she had little interaction with him other than business." Omar snorted.

"Nobody likes Eliza. Am I missing something?" Xander turned the ignition and pulled out of the lot.

"I'm glad you came to your senses and left her behind." Omar flipped through his pad. "Okay, this is what I've found. She knew Jeffrey well. They were seen together several times on the east side. She had the money, so we're tracking her credit card expenditures. It wouldn't surprise me if we find some hotel charges that won't be easy to explain," he paused and stared out the window. "Now, Olivia is a keeper. You had better put a ring on it before someone else does."

"She's got a ring. What we don't have is a date." Xander headed toward the east side. "But as soon as we're finished with this nasty business, I'm going to go hard on putting an end to that."

"Oh, you're going to back her in a corner, huh? I hope that bullshit doesn't backfire on you." Omar positioned his elbow on the armrest, and they rode a few minutes in silence. "You haven't told me where we're going."

"We're going to pay Ed an unexpected visit. Jaysa gave me his schedule. On Thursday mornings, he goes to the butcher shop to handpick his ground beef. We're going to have a conversation with him where we won't have to worry about being overheard."

Omar nodded. Xander could tell Omar had something on his mind, his talkative self hadn't shown up lately. But Xander had enough details crowding his head, he couldn't add Omar's baggage too. If Omar thought Calvin wasn't involved with drugs, he would find the evidence.

Xander whipped into the rear lot of the farmer's market. The structure was old and faded, but everyone in town knew it was the best place to get fresh produce, meat, and fish. The bakers had a reputation for best confections on the island. Maybe he'd take Olivia a dozen of those coconut chocolate chip cookies she loved.

He and Omar entered through a rear door of the market and snaked their way through the tight stalls and an assortment of aromas. This early in the day the co-mingled smells were too rich for his stomach.

They arrived at the rear of the butcher shop, and Xander glanced at his watch. "Ed should be here in a few minutes. According to Jaysa, this part of his routine is as regular as his morning bathroom routine."

Omar rolled his eyes and turned away.

At exactly eleven o'clock, the curtain parted, and Ed stepped into the back room dressed in his signature shirt with his name on the pocket and black pants. The moment he spotted Xander and Omar, he stopped. His startled expression was exactly the one Xander wanted to see. Caught off guard, he was more likely to talk.

Xander waved him in. "You might as well come on in here, Ed. We've gone through a lot of trouble to talk with you and we're not going to let you back out."

Omar walked across the room and stood behind Ed. Omar was taller and thicker than the slight man. He couldn't go around Omar, and Xander hoped he wasn't stupid enough to try.

Ed glanced over his shoulder. "Damn it. I don't have anything to say to you."

Xander motioned him forward. "We'll see."

"You can't keep me in here." Ed's eyes shifted around the small space. Xander's palms itched for Ed to take a run at him. He wanted to take a punch at the old man's worn face. Ed could have the clues to solve this mystery. Clamming up wouldn't work this time.

"We aren't keeping you against your will. You can leave any time you want, but we're going to talk to you. We can do it here or make a big scene at your pool hall or we can talk in front of your adoring wife... or at the police station." Xander stepped closer. "I know your car was parked outside my house. That will make for an interesting conversation, for certain. Your choice."

Ed clasped his hands. "What the hell do you want?"

"Tell us about Lawrence Cistos."

Ed's eyes narrowed as his face hardened. "I don't know who that is."

Omar shoved Ed with his shoulder. "See, that's what we're not going to do. We won't waste your time, so don't fucking waste ours."

Ed's lips formed a thin tight line. "How do you know about Lawrence?" He stared down at his shoes. His hands trembled enough to show his discomfort.

"We know you're lying. We have evidence that says otherwise," Xander said.

"If you have evidence, then what the hell is this all about?" Ed waved his arms around.

"We've lost three people over this bullshit. Either you talk, or we'll find a way to make you talk." Omar lifted his shirt to expose his Ruger.

"What are you gonna do, shoot me?" Ed yelled.

"If I have to. Don't give me a reason to, because I'm itching to unload some pent-up anger."

"Omar." Xander shook his head. He knew Omar felt as if he'd done something else or something different, Calvin would still be alive.

"Look, you don't want to know a lot about Lawrence. He's not a nice person. If he thinks he's been crossed, you'd rather be in a room full of scorpions." Ed moved away from Omar and closer to Xander.

"What are you doing for him?"

"Whatever he asks. I owe him and he called in the favor. I'm almost out from under."

"What favor did he do for you?" Omar asked.

"Money. He loaned me money to keep the hall open. The biggest mistake I ever made."

"Where can we find Lawrence?"

"New York."

"That's a big state. Narrow it down for us." Omar's voice was icy.

"Manhattan. East Side." He talked over his shoulder to Omar. "He's never invited me over for tea and I wouldn't go if he did. He's been fair with me, but he doesn't bullshit. When he called his note due and I couldn't pay in full, he started looking for other ways for me to repay the debt."

"Besides your cars, what else have you done?"

Ed looked down at his shoes again.

Another nudge from Omar made him lift his head. "I was a mule for him a few times."

"What'd you carry?" Xander asked.

"Heroin and cocaine." Ed changed positions. "Look, if he knew I was spilling his business, he'd kill me and maybe my family."

"We're almost done here. What do you know about the painting that Kais Bisset was trying to sell?"

"It belonged to Lawrence. He wants it back and nothing is going to stop him from getting it."

"Why is this painting so important? Why can't he go buy something else to hang on his wall?" Xander asked. "According to Kais, he'd changed his mind about who he wanted to sell it to."

Ed shook his head. "Man, you don't know who you're dealing with. If Lawrence thinks the painting is his, then it is. If someone is trying to keep him from it, then he's going to come harder. You can bet Lawrence's motive is deeper than something to hang on his wall." Ed glanced over his shoulder at Omar. "And it's going to take more than you two to keep him from what he wants."

Xander held up his hand. "Don't worry about us. How many people does he have on the island working on getting his painting back?"

"I've met four, but there may be more."

Xander was quiet for a moment. Ed was nervous, but he could be telling the truth. "Where are these guys staying? I don't imagine they're staying at the Ritz on the beach."

"I don't know for sure. We don't have in-depth conversations. My guess is they're in one of the rentals on the east side. There isn't a lot of scrutiny in that section of town and people don't ask a lot of questions."

"That's the best you can give me?" Xander studied Ed's face. His expression gave up nothing.

"What do you know about Jeffrey Greene?"

Ed lifted his chin as if he was trying to imagine the man. "You talking about the chump that is always hanging down at the beach? That surfer bum?"

"Sounds like you know him pretty well."

"I want to get something clear." He moved his hands in a crisscross motion. "I've never killed anyone for LC. That's where I would have drawn the line."

"No one is accusing you of murder," Omar said. "Just tell us what you know about him."

"Two-bit drug dealer. Sleazy. He talks a big game about how he's got a big network. I think he's just talking so no one will try to take his territory. I don't know anything else." He turned around to face Omar. "As soon as I get out from under LC, I'm done. I'm keeping my nose clean and running a reputable business. I want to retire and relax on the beach. That's what I came to Sebastian to do. Now can I get my beef and get the hell out of here before people start to get suspicious?"

"Remember, we know where to find you if anything you said doesn't check out." Xander stepped aside and motioned for Omar. They didn't talk on the way to the car. Xander was happy to be out of the confined space of the butcher shop and the overwhelming smell of raw meat. Omar strapped on his seatbelt. "What do we know now?"

Xander took a deep breath. "We know where Lawrence lives. We know Jeffrey sold drugs. And we know LC isn't going to open up to us about why he killed three people for a painting."

"We don't know that Lawrence killed everyone. Maybe he killed Kais, but Calvin and Jeffrey may be unrelated. Suppose what happened at the storage unit was a drug deal that went bad?" Omar tapped his index finger on the dash.

Xander nodded slowly. "That's a possibility." He started the car. "And where does Eliza fit in with all of this?"

"We need to figure that out."

Xander's phone rang. Olivia's name popped onto the console. He answered it through the car's Bluetooth. "Hey, Bae, what's up?"

"Luc's gone," she wailed.

CHAPTER 22

Olivia didn't know what to feel. Her body opened to every sad emotion. Her feelings were as foreign to her as the idea that Luc had been snatched. Miles, Alberta, and the police used the word kidnapped, but that was too dignified for what had happened to the cutest little boy she'd ever met. Even when he pouted about putting on his floaties, he looked like a miniature Xander.

She looked down at her legs. Her sarong must still be on the beach. If only someone had thought to bring it inside, she wouldn't feel naked and exposed right now. This was her fault. Fault. Fault. The word was pasted on her tongue.

"Is he here yet?" Olivia looked up from her hands.

"No, Olivia. I'm sure he's getting here as fast as he can." Miles tried to reassure her, but until she looked into Xander's eyes and didn't see blame then nothing was going to calm her.

"How could this happen? With all the people on the beach, wouldn't someone have said something? Wouldn't Luc have screamed for help?" She buried her head in her hands and cried fresh tears.

Miles' house was hot. All the people walking around taking notes and talking with each other sucked up all the cool air in the room. They had no idea that even though she only wore a swimsuit, her flesh was hot enough to melt cheese.

A police officer cleared his throat and kneeled on the floor in front of her. "Ms. Silva, can you tell me again what happened?"

"I told you everything I know. Saying it two hundred times isn't going to change anything. I was in the water rescuing Miles' grandson, Jason. When I came out of the water, Luc was gone. We searched the house, the road in front of the house, the beach in both directions. Please, start looking for him and stop asking me the same questions again and again."

Miles rubbed her knee.

"We have started searching. The more information you tell us, the quicker we'll find him. Please bear with us."

She heard a noise and sat up straighter. "Is that him? Is that Xander?" She looked to Miles again.

"No, it's another officer." Miles grabbed hold of her hand and tried to reassure her with a squeeze, but the only thing that would console her was Luc back at her side.

"What is taking so long?" She jumped off the chair. The crowded house was full of all the wrong people. The officers and detectives needed to do some real work, like find Luc.

"Where's Olivia?" The moment she heard Xander's voice, her heart started beating again. Until then, she wasn't sure what was keeping her alive. She rushed to the front room. Xander spotted her and opened his arms. She ran toward him and allowed his embrace to comfort her. A fresh batch of tears formed in her eyes and this time she didn't try to hold them back. Her body sagged against him, and she poured out the anguish she couldn't put into words.

"We're going to find him, Bae. Don't worry. I know we will." Xander allowed her to cry until she ran out of tears. They swayed slowly from side to side. The room quieted. The stares were obvious. Everyone watched them, studying their behavior, waiting to see if she'd fall apart. But she didn't care. He held her tight and allowed her to empty out the fear that consumed her.

When the sobbing subsided and her body stopped shaking, Xander said, "What happened, Bae?"

With her head resting on his chest, she fingered the button on his shirt and told him the details. She'd repeated them so often she was able to do it without breaking down. She would never be the same again, but with Xander by her side, it wouldn't be as painful.

"Is Jimmie here?" he asked.

"I haven't seen him." She lifted her head and glanced around.

He twisted without releasing her. "Omar, get Jimmie over here. Don't take no for an answer. I don't want a bunch of rookies working on this. I want him on it."

Omar withdrew his phone from his pocket and exited the house.

"Let's sit down, Bae." He led her to the chair near an officer.

"Can you answer some more questions?" The officer positioned his pen over his pad.

Xander held up his hand. "I have some questions. Have you questioned everyone who was on the beach?"

"Yes, sir."

"Have you knocked on all the doors in the neighborhood?"

"We're doing that now."

"Has a missing child alert been sent out?"

"One should be going out within the hour. Believe me, we're doing everything we can."

Omar walked back in the house and straight toward them. "Jimmie is on his way. He got the radio call and was heading over. I also called the crew. We're meeting at your place in two hours. I've asked them to do some digging before they arrive. Jaysa is on it, tracking intel."

"Olivia, did you see anyone on the beach today that looked out of place?" Xander asked.

She bit her lip and shook her head. "I can't say I was paying much attention to the others on the beach."

"How about you, Miles?"

Miles rubbed his hand together. "Xander, with four grandchildren here for a week-long visit before their parents get here, I've got my hands full. I didn't even notice when the youngest one put a booger on my shirt the other day. Now I know that Alberta and I are getting too old to try to manage them alone. This is all my fault. If Olivia hadn't saved Jason, Luc wouldn't be missing." His face fell as he swiped his eyes. "But Jason would have drowned." He added, before excusing himself from the room.

"I had to save Jason," she said to Xander. "This is all my fault. I was hoping Luc would have a fun day. I had no idea, this…"

Xander put his arm around her and drew her close. "Olivia, you had no choice. You did the right thing. I'm going to find the person who did the wrong thing."

"Eliza is going to blame me. She's going to kill me." She covered her mouth. "Oh, God. We need to call Eliza and tell her." Fresh tears surfaced as Olivia rocked back and forth allowing another unbelievable reality to set in. "Oh, God. Oh, God."

CHAPTER 23

Xander settled Olivia into the car. She needed to get home and rest. The longer she stayed at the scene, the more distraught she became. There was a wild look in her eyes that he feared would never go away. She rubbed her wrist over and over again as if she needed to erase something.

He closed the car door and started toward the driver's side. Jimmie approached from across the street, heaviness etched in the creases of his face.

"You've got to find Luc, Jimmie. There's no try. Find him alive." Xander's voice was marked with emotion. He wasn't thinking rationally. The pain was too sharp. Olivia was a wreck and he couldn't lose Luc. He just couldn't. The thought was a burden too heavy to carry.

Jimmie rested a hand on Xander's shoulder. The action was meant to calm him, but it had no impact. "I've got every available man working on it. I've even called in the two that were off today."

"My men are on it, too. I called in a few of my contacts. Ex-FBI. They'll arrive today."

126

Jimmie nodded.

"I might as well tell you now. I'm not going to play by the rules. So, if that's a problem for you, get the hell out of my way." Xander squared his shoulders.

Jimmie took a deep breath. "I didn't hear that, and I can't condone any illegal activity. But off the record, if it were my child, I'd do the same thing."

Xander drew back. Did Jimmie think Luc was his son, too? "I'm going to find him. I will." He turned away from Jimmie and climbed into the car. Olivia rested her head on the back of the seat. Her eyes were closed, but a steady stream of tears coursed down her cheeks.

He reached for her hand and squeezed hard enough for her to know he'd fix this.

Later, after he'd helped settle Olivia in bed, he sat in the chair behind his desk. He gripped his hair by the roots and squeezed his eyes so tight he saw flashes of color. But the act didn't erase the pained look on Olivia's face from his memory. Yelling would have felt better—helped him vent his anger, but Olivia was so devastated, she'd take his outburst personal.

At least the pills helped her fall asleep. For a few hours, she could rest. She looked like she was about to spin off into a black hole, constantly repeating the word fault. And no matter what he said, she wouldn't or couldn't stop.

He dialed Eliza's number again. By now, she should have called to check on Luc. Usually, when Luc was visiting, she called every few hours. It wasn't like her to go this long without demanding to speak to her son. After four rings, instead of going to voicemail, he received a message saying her mailbox was full.

He drew in a deep breath. The universe wouldn't be so cruel to allow him to find out Luc was his son only to lose him. The thought was too painful to hold. He dropped his head and exhaled through his mouth. "I'm going to find you, Luc. Hang in there, buddy. I will. I swear."

A tap on the opened door made him lift his head. Omar and Jaysa stood in the doorway of his office. "We didn't want to interrupt," Jaysa said.

He waved them in. "I needed a moment of quiet."

"How's Olivia handling this?" Jaysa propped her computer on the table and within seconds began tapping on the keys. The sound was comforting, now something was happening that he could control.

He shook his head to bring his thoughts back to the room. "She's resting. That's the only thing I can say." He tapped the tip of an eraser on the desk. "Jaysa, have you been able to pick up any activity on Eliza's phone?"

"No. Her phone pinged off a cell tower near the Teterboro Airport in New Jersey. She called a number I haven't identified yet." Jaysa punched a few more keys on the keyboard. "I can't find a number or any contact information for Lawrence Cistos. If he uses a cell phone, it must be a burner or registered to someone else. This man is a ghost."

"We know he lives in Manhattan on the east side. Maybe that will help you track him." Omar offered.

"Jaysa, see if Eliza's phone bounced off any towers in Manhattan," Xander paused while rubbing his chin. "What if Eliza didn't go to New York to handle final business for Kais? What if she went there to meet with Cistos? She called to pick up the painting before she left. Maybe she struck a deal with him."

"Did she tell you she didn't know Cistos?" Omar asked.

Xander looked at him. "She's been known to lie, but maybe he reached out to her."

"I've got something," Jaysa said. "Last night, her phone bounced off a tower on the east side of Manhattan. I can nail it down to a five-block area near the East River. It's a pricey area. Give me a couple of minutes and I'll have more information."

Olivia's phone vibrated across his desk. He'd taken it out of the bedroom so she could rest. "It's Adisa, the art shop owner." He hesitated before accepting the call.

"I'm sorry, I was trying to reach Olivia," Adisa responded when he said hello.

"Adisa, this is Xander. Olivia is resting. Can I give her a message?"

"I heard about Luc, Xander. I wanted to let her know I'm here for her."

"That information wasn't on the news. We're keeping it quiet for a few more hours." He looked at his watch. "How did you hear about it?"

"Miles told me in confidence. Look, Xander, something is troubling me and maybe it's better to talk to you than Olivia anyway. Mrs. Bisset picked up the painting yesterday, but she took the cheapest one of the three. She said she'd been in touch with the buyer. But the painting she took was not the one that Mr. Bisset told me his buyer wanted. I tried to tell her the difference, but she brushed me off. And this evening, a man came into my shop and roughed up my employee, demanding she open the vault. He ran off when a large group of tourists walked into the shop. I don't know what's going on, but I want those paintings out of my shop. I've heard whispers and I don't want any trouble. I have young children."

"How can I help you, Adisa?"

"Take the paintings. Get them outta here. I was doing Mr. Bisset a favor, and now he's dead. Can I sign them over to you and you can deliver them to his wife when she returns?" There was anxiety in her voice.

"I'll send a team down this evening to pick them up. Is that okay?"

"Yes, thank you. I'll get the paperwork ready."

"Can your employee describe the man that hassled her?"

"Oh yes, she can, and we got him on camera. We might be a small shop, but with the expensive pieces we carry, I have hidden cameras all around the shop. I'll pull the footage."

"Good, my team will want to talk to her when they arrive." Xander ended the call and relayed the information to Jaysa and Omar.

Omar extracted his phone from his pocket. "I'll send two men down to collect the art. It sounds like someone is getting sloppy, which means they could be more dangerous."

CHAPTER 24

Olivia opened her eyes. Xander thought she was sleeping, but no number of pills would accomplish that feat. At least now, her body was still and she had stopped crying long enough to feel the pain moving through her body. The thought of Luc with a stranger that might mistreat him, harm him, or even kill him numbed her from head to toe.

It was always like this. Something good came along, but the dreadful grip of disappointment or despair or denial swiped it away. And here she was lying in bed, crying while someone else went off to fight the battle to get Luc back. It was her fault he was gone, and she needed to help get him back.

She sat up and swung her legs off the bed. Xander had helped her out of her wet clothes and thankfully put them where she wouldn't have to see them. Her head felt as if it were stuffed with cotton balls. Everything was so surreal, even the smell of saltwater that still clung to her skin seemed out of place. She stood but flopped back onto the bed. After a moment, she took a deep breath and heaved her body forward.

It was time for her to find the strength to help Xander. If there was a chance Luc was still alive, she needed to do everything within her power to help find him.

The bedroom door opened. "I thought I heard you. Don't you want to rest a little longer?" Xander's voice sounded strained. His intense expression from earlier was gone.

She stood straighter. "I'm okay. I'm coming out to talk this through with you and the team. I might know something that might be important." Whatever was going on in her body, she needed to keep it to herself for now. Xander was worried about Luc, that was enough of a burden for him to carry. She wanted a partner she could share life with—the good and the bad. Xander's work was burden enough for him, he couldn't shoulder her worries, too.

"You don't need to do that."

She held his gaze. "Yes, Xander, I do." She managed to sound firm. "Luc was in my care and I'm doing this for me."

He held out his hand to stop her.

"Save it, Xander. I will shower and be in your office in fifteen minutes." She spun away from him. "Have you talked to Eliza yet? What did she say?"

"I can't reach her. She's not picking up."

"How can that be? Eliza always checks on Luc. By now, she should have called to tell him goodnight." She shook her head. The realization weakened her newfound resolve. "What does this mean?"

"I'm not jumping to any conclusion yet. I've got to stay positive."

"I'll be right out." Without waiting for him to approve or disapprove, she walked into the bathroom on steady legs and closed the door. She pressed her back against the cool glass of the shower before stepping in.

Fifteen minutes later, she walked into Xander's office with her anxieties covered in a cotton tank top and denim jeans. She didn't feel any better, but she needed to look tough enough to do what the rest of them did daily. Everyone glanced up when she walked in and sat in the chair in front of Xander's desk. "What have you found out so far?" She directed her question to Omar.

"We have the videos from the art shop and the nearby businesses," he said.

"What's that?" She pointed to the wrapped package leaning against the wall.

"The paintings Adisa was storing for Kais." Xander filled her in on Adisa's call.

She exhaled through her mouth to contain her fear. "Can we see the videos?" she asked Xander.

Omar booted up the video from Adisa's shop. A nondescript man with broad shoulders and a baseball cap with the brim turned backward walked into the shop and straight up to the salesclerk. The camera caught a good shot of his clean-shaven face. He said something to the clerk and nodded toward the back of the shop. She shook her head and started to walk away when he grabbed her shoulder and pushed her against the wall. He stood so close, she had to be intimidated. Olivia flinched. Even without the sound, the fear in the sales-clerk's eyes said she felt threatened. When she tried to pull away, he shoved her again, harder. Then their attention turned to the door as a group of tourists entered the shop.

"Snap a photo of that guy," Xander said.

"Already done," Omar responded. "Now, I'll fire up the footage taken from the businesses around the pool hall. Let's see if Ed told us the truth."

Olivia sat forward in her chair. The person who stole Luc might be in one of these videos. Maybe it was someone she'd passed on the beach or saw on the street. After a moment, she pointed at the screen. "There, there. It's the same man who was in the art shop."

Omar paused the video, and everyone drew closer to the computer. "So, we know it's one of LC's guys." Xander rubbed his chin. "Jaysa give me a list of all the rentals on the east side. Narrow it down to those that are occupied. I want to know who the property owners are and a list of who's renting."

"Gotcha." She pushed back to her computer and pounded the keys.

"I need it as fast as possible. How about an hour?" Xander said.

Jaysa gave him a severe stare. "I'll do the best I can," she said without changing her face.

Their landline rang in the house. Xander reached for the phone at the same time Olivia did. "I've got this, Xander." He didn't release his hand right away.

The voice on the other end of the phone was slow to respond. The background noises overwhelmed the caller's voice, making it almost impossible to make out what the woman was saying.

"Eliza, is that you? I can barely hear you," Olivia said.

Xander reached over and pushed the phone speaker button.

"Olivia, I need to talk to Xander."

It would have been easier to let Xander take over, but she was neck deep in this mystery and she wouldn't let him do this all alone.

"Talk to me, Eliza. Are you okay?"

"No, I'm not okay."

CHAPTER 25

Xander hunched over the phone. He wanted to put the receiver to his ear, but everyone in the room had stopped what they were doing to listen to the conversation. He signaled Jaysa without saying a word. By the way she assaulted the keyboard, she understood he wanted the call traced.

"Eliza, I'm here. What is going on?" Xander tried not to sound anxious.

There was a short pause where the only thing they heard were hushed voices followed by what sounded like a struggle.

"I have something you want, and you have something I want." The voice was deep.

"You have Eliza?" Xander modulated his voice.

"I have the mother and the son. Which is most important to you?"

Xander sat back in the chair. He caught Olivia's panicked expression. "This must be LC. Happy to talk with you finally." Xander switched on the friendly false voice.

"I want my painting. Sources tell me you have it."

"You're very thorough," Xander said.

"As are you."

"Where is Luc Bisset?"

"I don't think you understand me, Fitzgerald. I'm not negotiating with you."

"Until I hear Luc's voice, we aren't doing anything." Xander held his resolve. Again, there were hushed voices, but nothing he could make out.

"I'll get the kid and call you back." The line went dead.

Olivia jumped out of her chair. "Oh my God. They hung up. Why did they hang up? Have they hurt Luc?"

"Bae." He almost told her to calm down, but bit back his words. Under the circumstances, this was the calmest she could achieve. "They want the painting." He used his chin to point to the collection against the wall. "They won't do anything until they get their hands on that painting."

"Tonight? Will they call back tonight?"

He exhaled, making a small circle with his mouth. "I hope so. If Luc was in New York with LC and Eliza, he would have put him on the phone right away. Since he hung up, that means Luc is not there." He turned to Jaysa. "Call your contact at the airport. I want to know every non-commercial plane or helicopter that took off today. Whoever took Luc didn't use commercial air."

"What's first, that or the rental investigation?" she asked.

"I want to know if Luc is on the island. That's first," Xander said.

Olivia's face relaxed as she settled back into her chair. The room was quiet, even Jaysa seemed to hit the keyboard with a softer touch. Xander stared at the phone, willing it to ring for Olivia's sake. If he heard Luc's voice, his stomach would stop flipping. Sleep might not come, but he'd be able to close his eyes tonight.

When the phone rang, Olivia jerked forward in the chair.

Xander turned on the speakerphone. "Yeah."

"I wanna go home." Luc's voice was weak and hard to make out over his crying.

"Okay, buddy, I need you to be strong for me. You'll be home soon." Xander wanted to assure him. The child's crying tore him in two.

Luc muttered again, but it was indistinguishable over his crying. Then he was gone.

"You have my painting," LC's rough voice was back on the line. "You have forty-eight hours to deliver it to me here in the States. That's if anyone wants to see that little boy or his mother again. I'll call tomorrow with details." The line went dead.

Xander turned off the mute button, lifted the receiver from the base and settled it back in place. It was always good to be sure the line was dead. "Did you trace anything?"

"Nothing. It must have been a burner phone," Jaysa replied.

"Anything from Eliza's phone?"

Jaysa shook her head. "It's either off or the battery is dead."

"Why would Eliza go to New York with the cheapest painting? Was she trying to strike another deal? Did she think LC didn't know what he bought?" said Omar.

"How is she tied into all of this?" Olivia asked. "Why didn't she send LC the painting? Then none of this had to happen."

Xander nodded. "Yeah, the more this unfolds, the fouler it smells." He turned to Omar. "What have we found out about her and Jeffrey? Have you uncovered anything?"

"They were a couple, for sure. She checked the two of them into the Suites Hotel several times. She paid using her credit card, so discretion wasn't a priority. Their fling wasn't a big secret. If Kais cared about his relationship with his wife, then he had to be aware of the affair."

Xander blinked several times, letting the information find a comfortable place to reside in his head. Every time he thought he knew women, he found out he knew very little. Even Olivia, who had his heart, was still a mystery to him.

"Was Eliza on drugs?" he asked.

"Was she addicted? I don't know, but she dabbled. According to the hotel staff, she and Jeffrey often sat in their cabana on the beach and smoked joints." Omar looked pained as he relayed the information.

Olivia jumped out of her chair and almost toppled it over. "I took pictures while I was on the beach today. Maybe I picked up something in the background." She escaped from the room with relief on her face but was back within seconds with her computer.

While everyone buried their faces in computer screens, Xander stared at Olivia. She hunched over her computer with such intensity, her shoulders would ache in a few minutes. She blamed herself and he blamed himself. There were enough clues to guess something like this was going to happen. Eliza had told so many lies it was almost as if she'd become a stranger. She was hard enough to figure out when they were dating, he shouldn't have expected her to become less complicated.

"Look at these photos." Olivia placed her index finger on her computer screen.

Xander came to her side. Omar and Jaysa stood behind.

"See this group? They had to be sitting off to the left of us, but they have on street shoes. Who wears street shoes to the beach?"

A beach umbrella blocked the faces, but there were two pairs of workman boots. "I believe that umbrella was positioned that way on purpose. They had a clear view of you, but you had no idea what was going on with them," Xander said.

Omar reached over Olivia's shoulder and tapped her screen. "That's the same baseball cap we saw in the other two videos. It's hard to make out, since you only see part of it, but that can't be a coincidence."

Xander's breath caught in his throat. "Luc is still on the island and he's alive. They wouldn't take the chance of taking him off the island without a passport or any identification, and they'll keep him alive until LC gets his painting. So, we've got to work fast." The thought lightened the heaviness resting on his chest.

"That matches what my airport contact said. There were only a few planes leaving the island today. None of them met our criteria." Jaysa returned to her computer. "On the printout is a list of occupied rentals on the east side. I've highlighted the three most probable properties.

Olivia dashed to the printer and pulled off the sheets. She seemed prepared for a race. Her body was wired, reacting to every noise, every suggestion. Her eyes were wider than normal, observing her surroundings as if she needed to note every change, every detail. Such a high level of sensitivity was hard to maintain. The stress would make her sick. He'd seen this kind of reaction before—traumatic stress. Watching her was painful. He wanted to ease her pain. If he couldn't help her and get Luc back, then nothing else mattered.

He moved to her side and rubbed small circles on her back, hoping his love would give her a little comfort. "For the homes Jaysa has highlighted, start calling the property owners. See what they can tell you about the renters," he said.

"Who will I tell them I am?" Olivia looked up at him with those beautiful brown eyes and his heart tightened.

"Let me see." His thoughts went to bringing Luc home. "Tell them you're with the tourism board and you're doing research analysis to improve tourist traffic on the island. Omar, walk with me."

Once they were out of earshot, Xander said, "How many men do we have on the island?"

"A total of six. You and I make eight. I asked them to come in to help with the search."

"How do we stand with ammo?"

"We're stocked." Omar rubbed his chin.

"Can we roll tonight?"

"Check. All you need to do is make the call," Omar said.

Several minutes later, Olivia stuck her head into the kitchen and waved her hand. "Come back into the office. I think I've got something. I talked to the property owner. He said he has a short-term renter, but he couldn't provide any information. They paid in cash that was delivered by courier. The renter insisted on complete and total privacy."

Jaysa came to peer over Olivia's shoulder. "Yeah, this house is in the middle of nowhere. It requires a 4x4 to reach it. Its rental history is sparse because the condition isn't up to the normal quality that visitors to the island want."

"This might be the one." Omar pointed at the listing.

"Okay." Xander signaled for Omar to follow him again.

They exited the room, but Xander didn't speak until they were on the balcony overlooking the hill leading to the beach.

"Something's on your mind." Omar hung onto the rail.

"Put the signal out to the crew," Xander spoke low. A sophisticated listening device might pick up their conversation. "Assemble the crew and tell them to armor up. This isn't going to be easy. I think I know the area, and I want surveillance on the place now. Ears and eyes, I want to know how many people are there, and I want to know every word they utter."

"Why are you keeping this from Olivia and Jaysa?"

"Do you see the look on Olivia's face? She is inches from snapping in two. She doesn't need this much information. I'm protecting her."

Omar shifted his head enough to show disagreement. "She's not as fragile as you think, and she might not like the idea that you're keeping something from her. If you're going to be in a relationship with her, you had better find a way to be open and honest about everything. Everything."

Xander studied his assistant. "Why do you think you're an expert on marriage?"

"Not marriage. Relationships. I've been in enough of them. And I've gotten to know Olivia. She's not the kind of woman you put on a shelf. She's all in or she's out. Let her in."

He placed his hand on Omar's shoulder. "You're right. Gather the team and tell them we're meeting tonight. I'm sure everything we're doing is being watched. Don't take anything for granted. We'll meet at the warehouse at midnight. I'll fill Jaysa in on what's happening. She can monitor all the activity from a secure location."

Omar headed toward his car. Whatever happened tonight would be a whole lot easier to handle knowing Omar was by his side. This mission had to turn out okay. Olivia's sanity and Luc's safety depended on the expertise of Fitzgerald Security.

CHAPTER 26

Olivia sat crossed legged in the center of the bed. The quiet in their bedroom should have soothed her, but not tonight. Xander was in a state of perpetual motion. He seemed unable to sit down. Jaysa was staying overnight. Together, she and Jaysa were going to monitor the activity and read the schematics.

"How many rounds of ammo have you put in that bag?" she asked. This was the first time she'd watched Xander pack for a mission. Something dangerous like this was always sitting on the horizon of their relationship, which kept her stomach in constant turmoil. Ignoring the danger was getting harder to do. And this time, it was her fault. But he would make it right.

"It's better to have too much than not enough," he said without slowing.

"You've got enough for a small war," she yelled to him as he walked out of the room. She closed her eyes while she waited on him to return. Luc was okay. For now, he was okay. She held on to that nugget as if it was golden.

At the sound of his bare feet slapping against the bamboo

floors, she opened her eyes. "What's the plan?" she asked when he walked back into the room carrying a cache of unidentifiable tools.

"I need to get Luc out of that house before tomorrow morning. That's the only thing that matters. After that, things may happen that I can't control."

"What about Eliza? Is someone trying to locate her? Are you going to find her before morning too?"

He rubbed his chin. "I'm focused on Luc for now. He needs me more than Eliza does. She caused this chaos."

"I can't believe I'm the one saying this, but you've got to help her, too. I know she's done a lot—I mean a lot of stupid things, but she's Luc's mother. Suppose this guy decides to harm her? Luc could lose his mother and father. Think about Luc."

"I need the whole team right now to get Luc out," Xander said before walking out of the room again.

She tried to stay centered. If she kept talking, she wouldn't become unglued. Xander was almost the opposite. As tension mounted, he became quieter. She could almost see him connecting the pieces like a puzzle of what he needed to accomplish. He padded back into the room. "You have people in the States. You can instruct them to find her. You have ways. You narrowed down the location of this LC person and his properties."

He stopped and huffed out a big breath. "Eliza may not be in New York. If she double-crossed LC, he might have her locked up in a warehouse or a dungeon almost anywhere."

"If LC thinks you're going to focus on the island, she could be in one of his places. Maybe he's let his guard down with Eliza because you're so far away."

He rested his hand on his hip. "You're not going to let this go, are you?"

"She's Luc's mother." She never imagined she'd be

pleading a case for Eliza. There were more reasons to dislike her than to like her.

Xander studied her and shook his head. "I don't think I'll ever understand you. I didn't even think you liked Eliza."

"She's Luc's mother," she said again.

Xander reached in his pocket and extracted his phone. He threw it on the bed in front of her. "Call Omar. Tell him your sob story and see if he can make a call to New York."

She bounced on the bed. "You mean it?" she asked as Xander walked back into the closet.

"Yeah," he called out.

Ten minutes later, Xander came back into the room carrying his gun gear. He dropped the bag by the door. "What's that smirk for?"

"Omar agreed with me. He's already made a call to put a team on it. He even walked me through how I can help from here."

"What are you going to do?"

"I will use the tracking software on your computer to help the team maneuver through the two properties in New York that Jaysa identified. Mike wants me to give him an hour and they'll be in place."

He sat beside her, the mattress sagging underneath his weight. "Why don't you rest? You've been through so much today." He rolled the pad of his thumb over her cheek. His soothing touch settled her stomach.

She shook her head. "I can't. I want to do something to bring Luc home." Tears stung her eyes, but she fought them back. "Luc trusted me to take care of him. I was the one who should have protected him, and I didn't."

"But if you hadn't gone into that surf, Jason may have drowned. You did a good thing. No matter what, you did the best you could."

She dropped her head. He made sense, but it was impossible to see it that way. "Luc is not here." She spun her engagement ring around her finger. "I want to do this."

"It's stressful."

"Sitting here doing nothing is stressful, too. I won't be able to rest while you're gone. At least this will give me something to focus my attention."

He rolled his lip. She was set on what she wanted. There was no talking her out of this decision. He stood.

"Do you think I need to worry about an attack here at the house?" For the first time, doubt crept into her voice.

"Someone has been protecting the place for days. He's still on duty. You don't have anything to worry about."

She placed her hand at the base of her throat. "I…what… I…why didn't you tell me?"

"I didn't want you to worry. Now I wish I had someone following you, watching you along with watching the house." He pushed his hand through his curls. There in his eyes was the guilt he carried too. He blamed himself the same way she did. They always would. "Until I come back with Luc, I want you to keep your gun with you. I don't care if you're in the office, the kitchen or the bedroom. Know where it is and keep it near you. I've loaded it." Xander placed the gun in her hand. "I've got to meet the team. Tell me you'll stay inside, and you'll keep that near you?" He nodded to the gun in her hand. "This isn't a drill. If for any reason you need to leave, take the back stairs and walk through the thicket."

"I got it, Xander. Please be safe and promise me you'll come back, and you'll bring Luc with you." She placed the gun on the nightstand.

He pinned her on the bed and cupped her face between his palms. If their lives were blissful and loving like this every minute of every day, it would be a fairytale. But there was no such thing. "I have this under control, Bae. Trust me."

"But I do worry. Every time you strap on your gun, I

worry. I'm afraid as hell to set a wedding date because I can lose you at any minute. I don't think it's something I can ever get used to." There, she'd said it aloud.

"We don't live in fear, Bae. I've said it before, and I'll say it every day if I must. We take each day we're given, and we enjoy them together. I will protect you. Just do what I ask." Without giving her a chance to reply, he placed his tongue in her mouth and gave her a kiss that was full of the promise he'd just given her. The warmth and certainty of his touch was almost enough to make her believe him.

CHAPTER 27

Xander hoisted his weapon bag over his shoulder and made his way down the back stairs and into the thicket. Even though the sun had set hours ago, the warmth and humidity hung around. The weight of the bag made the hike to the access road difficult. The black shirt and pants absorbed the heat like a sponge. He was thankful for the long pants to protect his legs against the bougainvillea that he'd planted on purpose. Never did he think the plants would attack him. It was supposed to keep others away from the property.

With a deep sigh, he made it to the access road. And just as they'd planned, Omar waited for him.

Xander yanked open the back door of the sedan and threw his bag on the seat before climbing into the passenger seat with a thump.

"Not in as good a shape as you think, I see." Omar snickered.

Instead of responding, Xander buckled his seat belt and stared into the darkness. "Is everything in place?"

"Yep."

"Is my house still under surveillance?"

"Yep."

"How many are watching?"

"One car with two people inside. They have nothing to worry about. I put two men on your place." Omar started the engine and pulled away. With the headlights off, he made his way toward the main road, then turned them on.

They rode across town in silence. This would have been the ideal time to go over the plan, but Xander's thoughts were with Olivia. She feared a future with him. His faulty thinking had him believing anyone could live a happy life with him. But his occupation was dangerous. It was a burden he had no right to ask her to share. At least now he knew what blocked her from setting the date. And it wasn't something he could wish away. His occupation was a part of him, under his skin. He lived and breathed it just like he did Olivia. In his head, the two co-existed without difficulty. But in the real world, they might not.

Twenty minutes later, Omar pulled in front of the nondescript warehouse. They hauled the equipment inside. The six-man team already assembled in the room wore grim expressions. They were all dressed in black. These missions were never easy. There was no guarantee on the outcome. Xander walked to the center of the room. The computer screens glowed blue in the dimly lit room.

"Start talking, Danny. Time is not our friend tonight." Xander took the seat next to the tech geek. The others stood around.

"Earlier today, we sent a young couple to the house pretending they were interested in a quiet place to have sex. They said they thought the place was vacant and that they'd had sex last week there on the front porch. Before leaving, one of them managed to put a transmitter under the front window, then they stumbled off in a horny frenzy."

"Good ruse," Xander said. "What have you picked up?"

"There are two people inside and two guards outside, one in the rear and one in front of the house. They're all bored and want to get the transaction over. The air in the house works intermittently, so the heat has them cranky." Danny swiped the screen and another screen came into view. "There are three bedrooms, a kitchen, and a large great room. The two occupants in the great room are watching television—a ball game. Luc's in the bedroom on the west side of the house."

"How is he?"

"I think he's fine. They're telling him to stop crying and trying to ply him with ice cream."

Xander's heart constricted. Luc was always happy. It was hard to imagine him crying for so long. *He must believe the whole world has forgotten him.*

"They check in with each other every thirty minutes. That gives us plenty of time to do what we need." Danny continued. "There is a window in the bedroom on the back side of the house. If we take out the two guards, we should be able to get into that bedroom without anyone knowing. I figure we can take Luc out through the window and get him back into our vehicles. The two inside the house aren't a worry once we get Luc out."

"That sounds easy. Now tell me everything that can go wrong." Xander repositioned himself on the stool. "What about booby traps? They might have rigged the area around the house."

"We've considered that. We don't want to trip any wires or sound any alarms, so we're going to have to move slowly. We've already sent in an advance team. They're doing reconnaissance. We'll travel in pairs, one directly behind the next. Everyone remain alert and focused. These guys have got to be itchy, so they're going to jump at every sound.

"What if the two on the outside hear us and notify the inside crew? Even if they don't, what can we do to protect Luc? I don't want him to become a human shield," said Xander.

"Do you want us to disable the outside guards or take them out?" Danny asked.

Xander looked to Omar.

"It's your call," Omar said.

"I'm not an assassin. I don't want to kill anyone unless we're threatened. They're going to know we were the ones to rescue Luc, so if we pull this off, they'll come looking for us. Protect yourselves." Xander turned to face his team and made a temple with his fingers. "Disable the outside guards, tie them up. After I get Luc out of the house, I want the team to do the same thing for the inside crew, then call Jimmie and tell him what's going on."

Omar patted him on the back. "I've got Jaysa on the line. I'm going to put her on speaker. Listen up, everyone."

"Getting to the house is going to take some maneuvering. There is only one dirt road leading to the house and I'm sure it's monitored. The crew will have to park the 4x4s a quarter mile away and hike in. To arrive unnoticed, you must come in from the east. There are no windows on that side of the house and the brush will provide lots of cover," Jaysa said.

"Anything from the New York team yet?" Xander asked. Olivia must have picked up the extension. "Nothing yet. They've checked the facility closest to LC's condo and there isn't any activity there. They're checking the other place. I should know more in an hour," Olivia said.

"One more thing, Xander," Jaysa piped in. "Leave the earpiece in until the mission is over. With two operations happening at the same time, we'll need constant contact."

"I'll do the best I can. If I don't answer, it's because I can't," he said. "Is everything okay on your end?

"Yeah, no activity from the car. They're just watching the house. If anything changes, I'll notify you."

"Okay. The clock is ticking, so we need to get moving," he said before disconnecting the call. "We heard Jaysa. We'll need to scale down the gear. There is no way we can hike a quarter mile with all this gear. Just the bare necessities."

"Who's laying down the transmitter on the road? I don't want to be boxed in on the access road." Omar tapped his wrist.

Danny sat up straighter. "The advance team dropped the equipment starting a mile out from where we'll park the cars. If anyone comes in behind us, Jaysa will be able to pick them up and warn us. We've got everything covered."

Xander never doubted his team, but he wanted the details just in case they lost communication with each other. That's what was disappointing about Calvin. Maybe Xander hadn't been critical enough during the interview.

"Okay, let's get ready." Xander stood and moved to repack the duffel. When the team finished, they piled into two cars. Omar drove the lead vehicle. There were three of them in the truck and three guys in the truck behind them. Xander examined the aerial view of the house that Jaysa had sent by text.

"LC had to have help finding this property. Since he doesn't live on the island, he wouldn't know anything about this dump. Who do you think helped him?" Omar asked.

Xander rubbed his fingers over his forehead. "I'm unsure. Ed from the pool hall, maybe. I don't want to pile any more blame on Eliza unless I have proof. She already has enough things to explain."

Omar shook his head. "You have a soft spot for her."

"I like to operate on facts. Until I'm sure Eliza is involved, everything is circumstantial."

"Oh, Eliza is into this mess up to her ass. Open your eyes, man!"

They rode the remainder of the ride in silence. Pretending to study the plans in his lap was easier than responding to Omar. Xander swallowed the taste of blood on his tongue. Gnawing his bottom lip only made things worse.

Omar pulled off the main road onto the access road. The passage was narrow and overgrown with weeds and vines. Their pace slowed to twenty miles per hour as Omar navigated the rough terrain. Xander glanced over his shoulder to see if the other car was still behind them. With each bump over the tree-rooted road, Xander's resolve grew stronger. In a few hours, he would have Luc back in his arms.

"What do you think of Olivia helping Jaysa tonight?" Omar kept a firm grip on the steering wheel.

"I wish she was in Philly right now with her family. But that woman…" He shook his head.

"Yeah. That's what you love about her, isn't it? She's no *get-along-girl*. You definitely have a type." Omar slowed the car. "This is as close as we're going." Xander unsnapped his seatbelt and unlocked the door.

They exited the car and reviewed the plan once more. Four men were going to the house, two would stay at the cars and be prepared just in case. The summertime heat made his breathing laborious. Xander signaled for his team to follow him and started the trek through the brush.

He turned on his headset. "Let's get in position."

CHAPTER 28

Olivia stood over Jaysa's shoulder and watched the computer screen as instructed. The tracking devices in the cars showed every movement. It was like watching ants crawl across the screen. This time of night, traffic was light so crossing town wasn't an issue. The trucks were at the base of the hills. There were no mountains on Sebastian. The hills on the opposite side of the island were two hundred feet above sea level, but the terrain was rocky and overgrown.

"They stopped," she notified Jaysa.

"Now comes the hard part." Jaysa studied the screen.

"What do we do now?" Olivia tried to sound calm, but her heart wouldn't return to a normal rhythm until Luc and Xander were home.

"We watch and wait. Xander is wearing a transmitter in case I need to relay information to him."

The phone rang, and Olivia rushed to the desk. Her eyes fell on the gun and she pushed it away. "That's Mike," she said to Jaysa before picking up. She lifted the receiver with shaking hands. "Any luck?"

"There is a lot of activity in the unit. We're picking up several people. But we can't operate the same way you guys do on Sebastian Island. I can't blow the door off the entrance and charge inside. The southern district of Manhattan won't let us run our own operation without obeying laws."

"Do you think Eliza is okay? Will she be safe?"

"There is no way to tell. We're going in as soon as we get the all clear. I'll call as soon as we get sight of her."

Olivia hung up the receiver. The waiting was the hardest part. Most of the day had been spent waiting for something to happen, which should have been exhausting, but tonight the adrenaline pumping through her veins had her wired.

Jaysa waved her over to the table. "I've got them. They're out of the trucks and heading toward the house." She trailed her finger on the screen at the unidentifiable objects as they moved slowly through what appeared to be nothing.

Xander was probably in the lead. It was his nature. If they were going to meet trouble, he would be the one to encounter it first.

The phone rang again. Olivia dashed back and lifted the receiver. "Mike?"

"Bring up the blueprint of the building. There's too much traffic on the street to think about going in through the front door and too many people in the building for us to take chances. We need to get in unnoticed and scope out the situation. Our data says there are at least six people inside and intel says they're heavily armed. I think it's best if we go in through the rear. I hope there is some second story ductwork we can use to find out where they are in the building. Can you help me?"

She took the seat behind Xander's desk and scrolled through several images. It was hard to concentrate over her heart thumping against her ribs. Lives depended on the information she provided. If she could have, she would have called on Jaysa for help or to look over her shoulder, but Jaysa was so engrossed she almost had her nose pressed to the screen.

Olivia straightened in her chair. "I can do this," she muttered under her breath. Whatever her fears, she had to try. Xander was going into a dangerous situation, at least she had the luxury of sitting in a cool house. She swiped through each screen until she found the one that showed the outside of the building.

"Okay, Mike, there's nothing on the back of the building. Lots of windows but no vents. There are vents on each side of the building on the second floor." She trailed the schematic. "From the print, you can take it down to the first."

"How are we going to get into the second-floor vent? We don't have a ladder." There was sarcasm in Mike's voice.

"Well, I don't know." She hunched her shoulders not expecting to answer those finer details. Perspiration peppered her back. On the other side of the room, Jaysa talked into the mouthpiece, providing information to Xander's team. She'd done her analysis. Jaysa was the eyes for that team, seeing things they couldn't or didn't see. Olivia wished she was better prepared. It was her idea to find Eliza, now she was letting the team down.

"There are industrial sized dumpsters between the buildings on the east side. You'll have to use one of those to give you the lift you need."

"That will work." Mike sounded relieved. "Are you sure there are no obstructions? If we're outnumbered, I don't want any other surprises."

Olivia focused on the HVAC blueprint of the building. She had to get this right. There was no trying, only doing. In Xander's world, there was no room for mistakes. "No, you're good." She tried to sound like an authority, but the doubt was overwhelming.

"Can you stay on the line? It saves us some time. Just in case."

She agreed. Instead of daydreaming, she studied the different images, trying to foresee problems that the team could face. "Talk to me, Mike. Tell me where your guys are, and I can look out for you."

"We've entered the building and we're moving to the second floor." He whispered. "I hear an argument. I can't tell what it's about, but it sounds like infighting. Some type of double cross. We're going to drop down in the adjacent room and storm them. I'm going quiet."

She nodded as if he could see her. If staring at the computer screen all night brought Eliza home safely then she'd do it. Luc needed his mother and Xander needed Luc.

Jaysa waved her hands, drawing Olivia's attention. "Xander and the crew are near the house." She blew through her mouth and shook her hands as if to rid her fingers of cramps. "This is it."

CHAPTER 29

Xander pulled at the neck of his black t-shirt. The heat was getting to him. Sex every night and lush meals with Olivia had taken its toll. He wasn't in the shape required to trudge through the woods, carrying twenty pounds of gear in warm temperature. He threw his shoulders back and summoned his strength. He'd do anything for Luc. Even though the DNA test results were still days away, he knew how it would turn out.

The growth in the woods was knee high and thick. He smacked the back of his neck as an insect tasted him for a midnight snack. They were nearing the cottage, but it wasn't in view yet. "What's going on, Jaysa?" he spoke into the transmitter.

"It's quiet. No call from LC. And the New York team just breached the building where we think Eliza is held. After all this trouble, she had better not be part of this. If this is another one of her ploys, she may have to answer to me this time."

"Only after I'm done with her."

"You're getting close to the trips near the house," Jaysa warned.

"Thanks, I'll be in touch." He stopped and lifted his hand to get his team's attention. "We're getting close. This is where it's time to look for trip wires. They don't want to draw attention to the cottage, so it won't be anything too sophisticated. Send up the infrared drone and see if it can detect anything."

Lenny launched the drone, and Xander leaned over the screen making notations on where they needed to take care.

"My goal is to get Luc and slip him out the window. I'll be taking the direct line from here to there. The rest of you know what to do."

They nodded.

Xander continued down the incline. Thirty yards from the house, he motioned for Omar to slow again. Instead of the hurried pace of before, it was time to inch along. The first tripwire glowed green through the goggles. After inhaling, he stepped over the wire. One down, three more to go. He wiped his brow, and then signaled for the men to follow him.

As he neared the house, the trip wires were placed closer together. In the summer heat, the slow pace was excruciating. He wanted to hurry, so he could get out of the thorny brush, get Luc, and get back into the air conditioning in the comforts of his own home. With the cottage in view, hope bloomed in his chest.

Xander faced the men behind him and motioned for them to turn on their earpieces. "Everyone understand their position?" He maintained eye contact with each of them until he got the nods he needed. "Move out."

He and Omar were left alone. "Ready?" he mouthed to Omar.

"All day. Let's do this." Omar set off toward the house and

Xander had to catch up to him. Every time he went on a mission, his heart pounded faster as he neared the goal. But this time was different, his heart was in an uproar. He could feel the blood rushing through his body, pounding out his steps and his breaths.

"You've got company heading your way." Jaysa's voice rang in his ear.

"How far out?"

"They'll reach your vehicles in ten minutes, and then however long it takes them to get down to the house on foot."

"They must have known we were coming. What triggered them?" he asked.

"I have no idea. I'll check. But get moving."

"How many trucks?"

"One. Which means four men at the most."

"We got company?" Omar asked when he finished talking with Jaysa.

"At least four."

"We can handle them." He patted his weapons. "Let's get Luc and get out of here. I want to be on the other side of those trip wires before we run into them."

"Roger that," Xander said.

They reached the side of the house. The only sound was the mockingbird with its on and off again whistle. A shade at the window made visibility impossible. He lowered his gear to the ground and removed his M4 rifle, positioning it against the house. From inside his pocket, he slid out the plastic card to pop the window's spring bolt. If he pushed it up too fast, the sound might alert the shitheads in the other room or startle Luc. With painstaking slowness, he eased the window up and climbed inside. Luc was curled around a pillow with his eyes closed and his thumb in his mouth. Xander advanced to the lower bunk and positioned his hand over Luc's mouth. Luc's eyes flew open and he immediately tried to pull away. "It's me, buddy. I'm here to take you home." he whispered. Without waiting on a reply, he cushioned Luc into his arms and slid him out of the bed. The boy threw his skinny arms around Xander's neck and held on tight. He was still in his swimsuit. He wouldn't make it long in the thicket behind the house without any protection for his skin. The sooner they got him to the car, the safer he'd be. At the window, he handed Luc to Omar who started back the way they came without saying a word.

Xander climbed out the window and followed close behind Omar. One hundred yards from the rear of the structure, after he was sure Omar could make it to the vehicle, he spoke into the transmitter. "Target is safe. Move in."

He crouched in the brush and waited for the action. Within moments, shouts ripped through the night air, and then gunfire drowned out everything else like fireworks. Omar's head start back to the access road should keep him and Luc safe. Now that he didn't have to worry about the tripwires, he could move faster.

Xander stared at the window of the small bedroom. It didn't take long for him to hear the bedroom door burst open and a face to appear in the open window. "He's gone," the kidnapper yelled into the room. The man hoisted his legs through the window and landed on the ground. Xander waited to see if the other man inside would follow, but the first man through the window was advancing fast. The gunshots and noise in front continued to pierce the air. Xander used the bush for cover. He cushioned the M4 rifle against his shoulder. Through the scope, he pointed the muzzle at the kidnapper's chest. "Stop right there," Xander yelled.

The kidnapper lifted his gun and continued to charge. Without slowing, he aimed his gun and pulled the trigger. A volley of bullets whizzed by Xander's ear and landed behind him, pitting the undergrowth. Xander steadied his rifle and hit the target in his right shoulder. The impact jerked him to one side, but the man kept advancing. Xander pulled the trigger and landed two shots to the center of the chest. The kidnapper dropped to his knees and fell forward. Xander glanced back to ensure no one else would come bounding through the window. After a moment, he made his way to the man. A dark pool of blood oozed from the gaping wound in his chest. Xander inched away from the house. Omar might need his help.

"I've got one suspect down. Tell me what's going on in the front." Xander spoke into the transmitter.

"We've got one inside with a lot of firepower."

"There is company coming in on the access road, as many as four. Omar and I will take care of it. Signal me when you've got an all clear. We might need help."

CHAPTER 30

Olivia shifted in Xander's chair and rubbed her burning eyes. Jaysa was absorbed in her computer screen and listening to the activity coming through her transmitter in case something important came up. Mike hadn't called in several minutes, but Olivia wanted to be ready for any questions. She wanted to prove she could handle the assignment. She tapped her nails on the desk to keep her focus.

"Are you bored?" Jaysa asked.

"Far from it. I don't know how you do this. I'm so tense, I can't hold an intelligent thought."

"It takes practice."

Olivia glanced at the computer screen, and then back at Jaysa. "To take a good picture, I have to have a lot of patience. Waiting for the right light, the right shadow, the right smile or the right something. That waiting is peaceful, almost cleansing. This waiting makes me crazy."

Jaysa's eyes sparkled as if she understood Olivia, then she dropped her head back to her computer. The quiet returned, but Olivia wasn't used to the stillness.

"Xander just communicated, they have Luc and are on their way back to the cars. The situation is under control." Jaysa pumped her fist.

Olivia fell back against the chair and held her hand to her throat. "Thank God." The nightmare was over. Tension and stress oozed from her body like the tide away from the shore. Now Xander and Luc needed to get home. The moment she could look into their eyes and know for sure they were safe, she'd let total peace envelop her.

The overwhelming relief that flooded her chest was the best feeling she'd had in days. From the moment Eliza offered her house for their wedding, the Bissets had dominated their lives. Those people were like a bad luck charm that had no off switch. At least now Luc was safe, and if Mike could locate Eliza, Olivia would be able to take a breath that wasn't coated in fear.

A popping nose outside drew her attention. She strained to decipher the sound. "Do you hear that?"

"Yeah. What is it?"

"I don't know." She pushed away from the desk and stood. "I'll check." She started toward the door.

"Take the gun."

She rolled her eyes at Jaysa but grabbed the weapon. "Thanks." She clutched the Glock at her side. The moment she walked out the door, the house went dark.

"What the hell happened?" Jaysa jumped up.

"Don't worry. Xander has people guarding the house."

Jaysa adjusted the transmitter in her ear. "Xander, electrical power is out at the house. Olivia's getting ready to check it out." Jaysa listened for a moment. "He says the guys outside should be able to check it out for us."

Olivia made her way to the front windows. From her location, she couldn't see the cars that were watching the house, but she expected to see Xander's men coming up the lane. Only, there wasn't any activity outside. Unlike the city of New York, she couldn't glance out a window at her neighbor's house to see if power was out in the entire section. Trees surrounded this side of the house. But from the balcony, she could see down the hill to the Macklemore house. With her gun resting at her side, she made her way toward the balcony.

"Olivia, Xander wants to know what you're doing?" Jaysa called.

"Tell him I'm trying to see if his guys are checking on us. I don't see any activity outside and I can't tell if this blackout is just our place or the whole neighborhood."

"He said do not go outside and do not open any doors. He should be here in twenty minutes."

"Does he expect us to sit in the dark until he returns to rescue us? That's not how I want to live my life. Standing in his shadow waiting for him to come to my rescue," she said under her breath.

From where she stood, she saw two men climb the stairs of the balcony. They weren't with Fitzgerald Security. Panic and fear rose in her chest like an inferno. "Jaysa, take your computer and go to the theater room. Now!" she yelled.

She backed away from the large glass doors. From the shadow of the house, she scrambled behind Jaysa. Once they were inside the room, she threw the lock and immediately keyed in the code to the vault. "Have you ever used a gun?" she asked Jaysa.

"Hell, no. Like I said, I'm a computer geek. Xander pays me good, but not this good."

"Tell Xander I don't know what happened to his men, but two strangers are approaching."

Jaysa reached for her ear. "Damn it. I must have dropped the transmitter." She patted her clothes.

Olivia removed a small Ruger from the vault and slipped

bullets into the chamber. "Well, take this gun. It's loaded, so don't point it at anyone you don't want to shoot, especially at me. If anyone breaches that door and they don't identify themselves, shoot as if your life depends on it. It might."

"Where are you going? You're not going to leave me here alone, are you?" Jaysa's eyes were wide with fear.

"I will do what I can to make sure we stay alive until Xander and Omar get here. If I stay locked in here with you, we'll be easy targets. They're probably coming for the painting and that's the only thing we can use to bargain with them. I need to get them and secure them in the vault."

Jaysa bit her bottom lip. A little over a year ago, she was in Jaysa's place with the same look of fear in her eyes when Ajay attacked her. "Hey," she said, "we can handle this. Now lock the door."

Olivia stepped through the door and listened until the lock engaged. The house was quiet. The darkness made it feel threatening. She inched along the wall, containing her breathing. If anyone were inside, the sound would give her away. The massive sound of crashing glass startled her. She crouched low. They were inside. She didn't have the training for this. Her hands shook so much, the ability to shoot a target was doubtful.

Xander's office was only a few feet away. She needed to make it there, some of the furniture would provide cover. She crawled along the outer edge of the hall, careful not to make a sound. With the Glock in her hand, she had to be careful. When she heard footsteps on the crushed glass, she hurried. Just ahead, she saw Jaysa's transmitter on the floor.

On hands and knees, she took a deep breath and picked up the transmitter before scurrying into the office. She eased the door closed. "Xander are you there?" she whispered.

"Can't talk now. We've got company." Xander's tone was clipped.

"But…Xander…someone is in the house."

There was no response.

Footsteps grew closer. They weren't trying to be quiet. She pushed the paintings behind the desk, careful not to make a noise, but the wooden frame of the biggest picture bumped the desk and the sound rang out like a thunderbolt. She froze.

"Xander, are you there?" She wanted to yell into the transmitter but couldn't. There was no sound coming through. Xander wasn't there. He wasn't there. *He wasn't there!*

CHAPTER 31

Xander caught up to Omar, who couldn't move as fast with the forty-pound weight of Luc in his arms. Somehow, the night had grown hotter, and his t-shirt was soaked through. When he drew close to Omar, Luc lifted his head and stared at him with eyes so sad his heart ached. Luc reached out to Xander and began to squirm in Omar's arms.

"You might as well take him."

"I can't. I'm the better shooter. I need to lead the way just in case. Luc, let Omar carry you. I will get you back to the house as soon as I can. You've hung in there this long, just wait a little longer. Okay, buddy?"

Luc placed his head on Omar's shoulder but said nothing.

Xander stepped in front of Omar and advanced up the hill. "Stay low."

The going was a lot easier than the coming. With their precious cargo under his protection now, Xander felt invincible. He made it to the trip wires, lifted his hand to signal Omar, then trounced the wire and moved forward. With the night vision goggles in place, everything was neon green and fuzzy around the edges. It was difficult seeing in the thick bush, but it was quiet enough to hear the footsteps crushing the tree limbs that littered the path. Xander stopped and pushed the goggles onto his forehead. "We've got visitors, we might as well wait here for them. You take Luc and go right. That's far enough out of the way, you might not see any action. I'll settle here."

Omar gave him a long look. "I'm not sure we should separate. We'd make out better together."

"Under any other circumstance, I'd agree with you. But I can't put Luc in danger. No matter what happens, you get him back to Olivia and Eliza."

Omar didn't say anything, but Xander could tell he didn't agree as he trudged in the opposite direction. Luc whimpered, but the decision was the right one. Xander readjusted his goggles and planted his rifle on his shoulder. Between the night birds and the katydids, the lush timberland sounded like a symphony. The singing could have lulled him to sleep, if the mission wasn't so crucial, but not tonight. The happy sound bouncing off the lush foliage didn't negate that danger was only a few feet away.

Xander narrowed his gaze, studying the terrain. The margin of error was slim to non-existent. With Kais gone, Luc needed to get back into a stable environment before he started to suffer from irreparable damage. Olivia was right to insist they find Eliza.

Xander jiggled the transmitter. "Olivia, are you there?" He waited for a reply.

"Danny, can you reach Jaysa or Olivia? I'm not getting any communication from them." Danny didn't reply either.

Every maneuver was all about the details. The transmitters were supposed to work, and they should have anticipated another team coming in behind them. There was no margin for little mistakes like this. Olivia and Jaysa had to be in trouble. He needed to get to them. Now.

Xander crawled forward on his stomach. Something was wrong somewhere. He needed to get out of this jungle and check on the people that were important to him. He heard the entourage before he saw them. Walking through the bush without making a sound was impossible. He could yell for them to give up. But these guys were paid to complete a task, no matter the consequences. There would be no surrendering, only a pile of dead bodies. He fired a round of shots into the ground in their direction. Three men dropped to their knees and started firing back. These guys weren't a bunch of weekend warriors.

Xander rolled away and landed on a bayberry bush. Thorns tore through his shirt and pierced his back. "Damn it," he mumbled.

The goggles slipped, and he readjusted them to locate the group clustered together. They were easy targets to pick off. Through the gun's scope, he narrowed on one and blew a hole in his head. "That's for you, asshole."

The thicket remained quiet. For a nano-second, all activity ceased and then a volley of rapid-fire gunshots filled the air. The sound of bullets hitting the trees and ground was deafening. Xander ducked his head, burying it under the protection of his arms. The smell of dirt filled his nostrils as he flattened his body against a tree.

When the firing stopped, he straightened his goggles and lifted his head. There was no movement from the direction the bullets came from. He steadied his body to detect the sound of movement.

"Fitzgerald," his name rang out in an ominous tone, "I have something you want."

Xander sat up with the rifle balanced against his shoulder. "What I want is for you to give up. You're not getting out of this the same way you came."

"You're not in a position to negotiate."

"That's where you're wrong. Under the right circumstances, everything is always negotiable. So I'm done talking."

Ten yards in front of him the leaves parted, and a man stepped forward. Xander raised his rifle and started to cock the trigger. Then he saw Luc. Mud smudged his face, but his tears had cleared a path down his face. His legs dangled and his bare feet kicked without impact.

"I wanna go home," Luc cried.

Xander took his time getting to his feet. He removed the goggles and dropped them at his feet.

"I wouldn't do anything stupid, Fitzgerald." The man hoisted Luc higher against his chest. "Drop the rifle and kick it over here."

"I wanna go home." Luc wailed again, louder this time. His bottom lip trembled as his eyes pleaded for what Xander couldn't give him.

"Hang in there, buddy. This will be over soon." Xander tried to assure him.

"Yeah, all we want is the painting. Then this can be over."

"Where is Omar?"

"He's indisposed right now." The man stepped forward. "That's enough pleasantries. Time for business." He turned his head. "Hey 'T' are you ready?" He called over his shoulder.

Two men walked out of the bush. "He won't be any trouble."

"Is Omar hurt?" Xander demanded.

"You've got enough to worry about right here." He shifted Luc forward to draw Xander's attention.

They advanced on Xander. One coming from the right, the other from the left. He didn't have much time. In one swift move, he retrieved his revolver from his back pocket and shot the man holding Luc between the eyes. Luc hit the ground hard. Xander shot the other man, and the bullet grazed his neck. Before the man could level his gun, Xander shot him again. The kill shot opened his head. Xander pointed his gun at the last man, but it was too late. His heavy boot caught Xander's chin. He placed his forearm around Xander's neck in a choke hold. "The only reason you're not dead, is because we want that painting. Otherwise, I'd kill you." His breath was hot.

Xander struggled to breathe as he lost his bearing. He braced his back and heaved his assailant several feet away. His revolver had to be near. He patted the ground until he felt the muzzle of the gun in the tall grass behind him. Before he could right himself, the man landed a punch to his kidney, sending a spasm of pain through Xander's body. He stumbled as his vision blurred. Using Xander's pain to his advantage, the man climbed on his back and tried to wrestle the gun from Xander's hand. But the gun was the only thing keeping him and Luc alive for now. His fingers landed on the gun grip. Without hesitation, Xander flipped the man over, pointed the pistol and fired off several shots into the man's chest.

On his knees, Xander continued to gasp for air. He didn't have much time. He came to his feet and made his way to Luc. "Are you okay?"

Luc didn't answer. He closed his eyes and cried. Xander lifted the boy into his arms and Luc's small arms surrounded his neck. The clammy feel of his skin was as worrying as the constant crying. "Let's find Omar." He rubbed his palm over Luc's back. "Everything is okay now, you can stop crying."

Xander yanked the transmitter from his ear and tossed it on the ground. The mosquitos buzzed by his ear, feasting on his blood like a buffet.

"Omar," he yelled his assistant's name. There was no response. He concentrated on the ground. Mindful of nothing protecting Luc in his swimsuit, Xander swatted away the branches that would have scratched the boy's delicate flesh.

Omar was slumped against a patch of young bamboo trees. He ran to Omar, who didn't move. "I'm going to put you down now, Luc. Just let me check on Omar." The boy tightened his hold on Xander.

Without releasing Luc, he settled on his knees and pressed his index finger to Omar's neck. His pulse was weak, but he was alive... for now.

The spot of blood below Omar's stomach grew. He needed medical attention. "Luc, I need you to be a big boy for me." Xander spoke slow, trying to console the boy. "Omar needs my attention right now. Can you help me?"

Luc nodded but didn't release Xander's neck.

"We need to get Omar to the hospital. We're going to help him just like the superheroes we are, right?"

Luc nodded again.

"I will carry Omar and I want you to hold on to my belt. Promise you won't let go, okay?"

Luc's eyes were larger than normal. The idea of being heroes must have appealed to him. Luc loosened his hold on Xander and placed his feet on the ground. Xander pulled his shirt over his head and handed it to Luc. "Put this on. It's too big, but it will protect you from the bugs and the bushes.

Xander picked up Omar and settled his limp body over his shoulder. With Luc holding his belt with one hand and his thumb in his mouth with the other, they started the trek to the car. Luc's short legs made the journey slow and hot and heavy. The cut above Xander's eye stung and blood trickled along his jaw. Exhaustion consumed him, but this wasn't the time to give in. There would be time to rest later. Maybe.

CHAPTER 32

Olivia crouched on all fours just beyond the desk. She couldn't move. Didn't want to move. Fear gripped her, holding her in place like cement. This whole thing needed to come to an end. Her body beyond tired, she was so exhausted. Her limbs felt like they belonged to someone else and mustering the strength to control them seemed unreasonable. She pulled her cell phone from her pocket and dialed Jimmie, but the call went to voice mail?

"Jimmie, I need you at the house. Someone has broken in. Please hurry." The words rushed out in a hushed tone. "Hurry!" She added, ending the call with a prayer that he would get the message and come as soon as possible.

"You might as well come out. We know you're in here. If you make us find you, we'll be mad as hell." A heavy voice yelled to her.

She flopped on her butt and inhaled. They weren't sure yet where to look. There was no place in Xander's office to secure the paintings, and she couldn't make it back to the theater room. It was too late. They were in the house.

"I'm not going to warn you again." They were getting closer.

She shoved the paintings under the desk. Not sure why she even bothered. If she handed them over, maybe the intruders would leave. But so many lives had been destroyed because of them, she needed to do what she could to protect them. The paintings were the reason Kais was dead, Luc was kidnapped, and Eliza was in trouble.

Time stopped. Every sound in the house echoed. Her breathing was accentuated along with every other noise. Hard boots pounded against the bamboo floor.

With her back against the wall, she sat facing the door. The gun leveled in her trembling hand. If Jaysa stayed in the safety of the theater room, she was confident she could handle this situation.

The footsteps faded. They weren't coming this way. Relief didn't blanket her. They hadn't changed their minds and decided to leave, they were going deeper into the house, which meant Jaysa could be in trouble. Olivia scrambled to her feet and tiptoed to the door. She eased it open and listened. Jimmie should be here by now.

She closed her eyes and whispered a prayer. They were pounding on the locked theater door. Jaysa was the unknown. There was no way to know what she would do. When it came to computer or technical gadgets, she could land a person on the moon with a rubber-band and a shoestring, but when it came to shooting, she was about as competent as a two-year-old.

Olivia came out of the office and inched her way around the living room. She was comfortable with her camera, not with the Glock. The weight was heavy and awkward. Two men stood at the theater room. One on each side of the door. If Jaysa shot through the door, she wouldn't hit either one of them.

Olivia got down on her belly, trying to imagine what Xander would do. She knew enough to make herself as small as possible. She shifted. If she was going to take a shot, it had to count. Shooting at a black silhouette was nothing like shooting at a person. Her hands shook, making it impossible to narrow in on the target. Her father always said if you're going to shoot someone, you had better try to kill them. Now, faced with the circumstances, she couldn't aim at the chest or head. Killing was final, there was no returning to normal if she killed someone. She took a quick breath and peeked around the corner. She aimed at the thigh of the closest intruder and pulled the trigger.

Both intruders turned and charged her. Instead of one of them dropping the way she'd hoped, they looked angrier. She aimed again, leveling the gun higher this time, but she missed. "Shit." She made her way to the front door.

Strong hands grabbed her shoulders and threw her backwards with so much force she bumped her chin on the floor and the gun flew out of her hand. Pain shot through her jaws.

"Get the hell up," the tallest one yelled before crashing his fist into her jaw. Colors flashed behind her eyes. The kick to her side made her struggle to gather her bearings. Standing seemed impossible with the pain consuming her. The same thug grabbed her arm with claws like steel and yanked her to her feet. She heard it pop, before she felt it. Pain radiated down her right arm.

"Where is the painting?" Another voice yelled from somewhere in the house.

She blinked several times, trying to focus on the two men in front of her. The burly men were enormous. One was over six feet tall and seemed just as broad. Either one of them could snap her in two with little effort. Their menacing faces made movement impossible. As hard as she tried, she couldn't form a word. The pain made it impossible to focus on anything else.

"Where is the painting?" the shorter one barked.

She clamped her mouth shut. Anger flashed in his eyes, then he slammed his fist into her jaw. The blow sent her flying across the room like a rag doll. Instead of getting up, she stayed on the floor and curled her body into a ball. Whatever happened, she couldn't defend against it.

The sound of gunfire erupted in the room. She closed her eyes and prayed whatever came next was less painful than what had already happened. Her face hurt, her shoulder throbbed, and her ego hurt. She was supposed to shoot to kill. She hadn't come close.

CHAPTER 33

Xander glanced at the plain black and white oval clock on the waiting room wall. The long hand dragged around the face as if it was stuck in another decade. By now a doctor, a nurse, or even an intern should have come out of the exam room and given him an update on Omar's condition. He ran both of his hands through his hair.

The sun settled high in the sky with the dawn of another day. With all the destruction that had taken place in the last twenty-four hours, greeting a new day was a mountain too high to climb. Nothing was settled. There was still much left to do, and so many questions needed answering.

He needed to talk to someone. The isolation of the hospital was suffocating. He pulled his phone from his pocket and dialed Danny. "What the hell is going on? Haven't you guys secured that scene yet?" He barked into the phone. His patience evaporated.

"We're pulling out now. This scene is secure." Danny was preoccupied with something.

"I can't reach Olivia. I want you to go to my house now

and check things out. Call me as soon as you find out something. Don't leave me flapping. I need to know now."

"Will do, boss. How's Omar and Luc?"

"The doctor checked Luc out. Physically, he's fine. He might have to talk with a therapist. No word yet on Omar. He wasn't too good when I brought him in. Now get to my house."

He disconnected the call and wrapped his arms around Luc. He'd fallen asleep on the ride to the hospital. The intermittent whimpering continued even though he wasn't awake. Xander rubbed Luc's back. The swirling motion calmed the boy's cries and eased the stress raging through Xander.

Instead of sitting in the waiting room, he should have gone home to check on Olivia. Being needed in two places at once was a new feeling. Unsure if he liked or disliked the tug was hard to determine. Until Olivia, no one could have convinced him that anyone would matter that much to him. But the list kept growing. Now Luc occupied a more special place in his heart.

The guilt of putting Olivia and Luc in jeopardy straightened his back. Starting with Luc. He dialed the paternity lab. Waiting for an answer about Luc was an unnecessary obstacle. Eliza could have told him the answer.

It was too early for anyone to be in, but when the recorder came on, he said, "This is Xander Fitzgerald. I dropped off a sample for a paternity test a few days ago. I don't care what it costs, I want to speed up the results. I want them as soon as possible." He ended the called and settled back in the chair.

A woman with hospital scrubs walked into the waiting room and over to him. He didn't have the strength to stand. From the grim expression on her face, he inhaled and braced his back against the chair.

"You're here with Omar Stewart?"

"I brought him in. How is he?"

"He's resting for now. We've put him in an induced coma to ease the pain. I can't tell you more since you're not the next of kin. You might as well go home and rest. There's nothing you can do here."

"Can I see him?"

She shook her head. "Only family." She placed her hand on his shoulder. "I'll call you if something changes, even though I'm not supposed to." She tipped her chin toward Luc. "He needs to get some rest." She stepped aside as if she intended to escort him out the building.

Xander cradled Luc in his arms and made his way to the parking lot. Each step weighed on him. Leaving Omar was the hardest thing he'd done all day, but Luc needed his attention also. Until they were able to find Eliza and get her back home, Luc was in his care. His responsibility. It was bad enough he had to endure the kidnapping.

Outside the hospital, Xander blinked several times while his eyes adjusted to the sunlight. The hospital gown flapped in the morning breeze. Luc stirred in his arms but didn't wake. Xander settled him in the back seat of the truck and secured the seatbelt. He took one last glance at the hospital before he turned the ignition and pulled away. Omar would understand.

It was too early in the morning for traffic to clog the streets. Xander shook his head. This mission had gone so wrong. His team was better than this. They needed to regroup and evaluate every step.

He turned onto his street and his heartbeat sped up. Two cars clogged the street near the lane leading to his house. He pulled over far enough away from the house to not be seen. After wrenching his gun from the glove box and shoving it into his pants pocket, he hoisted Luc into his arms and carried him to the neighbor's house. He leaned on the doorbell until his neighbor answered. Margaret yanked the door open, her mouth twisted in a frown. Her hair stuck straight up, and from the way she fastened her robe, it was likely she'd been sleeping. Without waiting for her to speak, he shoved Luc into her arms. "Watch him for me. I'll be right back."

He started off the porch.

"Xander, what the hell is going on?" she called to him.

"Margaret, I can't talk now. Lock your door and don't come out until I come back."

From the pit of his soul, he gathered strength and sprinted down the hill. At the house, he pressed his back against the tree. Whatever he was going to do, he needed to do it fast. He shifted to see around the tree.

He took two deep breaths, then pressed his body against the house for a moment before charging up the porch stairs and through the door.

Olivia lay in a fetal position on the floor. He ran to her and dropped to his knees.

"Are you hurt?" The sound of his voice seemed to soothe her enough to ease the shaking. She looked into his eyes, relief flooding her face. "What happened here? Are there intruders in the house?" Xander said, his hand still on his gun.

"I don't know. I don't think so." She tightened her good arm around him.

Danny and two men from his crew ran through the front door with guns drawn.

"Check the house. Make sure we're all clear," Xander barked without releasing Olivia.

Two men charged toward the back of the house, leaving Danny.

"What took so long for you to get here?" Xander said.

"We were on the opposite side of town in the sticks,

remember? We got here as soon as we could." Danny glanced over his shoulder.

"Where are the police?"

"We had the whole squad at the shack. Hell was breaking loose." Danny shrugged. "I've called for a medical unit. I'll be outside if you need me."

Xander pulled Olivia free. Her bruised face and swollen lips were too much. "Bae, talk to me." He'd put an end to this. Someone would pay.

CHAPTER 34

The best thing she'd seen in a long time was Xander. Her body riveted with pain. Even the tips of her fingers ached. With this much discomfort, the trouble going on around her was nothing. His arms cradled around her, which meant she was safe. The pain would stop. She held onto him with a grip so tight, he couldn't pry her fingers loose. As long as she clung to Xander, she'd be okay.

"They took the paintings. I tried to get them into the vault, but there wasn't time." She spoke in a whisper because there was no stamina to talk louder.

"Don't worry about that. It's not important." He cradled her close.

"Is Jaysa okay?" She wanted to lift her head, but the throbbing was too intense.

Xander's eyes shifted to the living room entrance.

"I'm here. I stayed in the theater room like you said." Jaysa rounded the corner and took a seat on the sofa. "You look like shit, Xander."

"I feel like shit, so my appearance is fitting."

Olivia struggled to sit up. Her head pounded like an army of drum majors were inside. She released Xander and placed her palms at her temples, then noticed the bandage on Xander's forehead. He wore a hospital gown and a large circle of blood stained his shoulder. "What happened to you? You're hurt." She started to reach for his shoulder but drew her hand away. The blood was fresh. She sat up straighter. "Where's Luc?"

"Take it easy, Olivia. We need to get you to the hospital."

"Where is Luc? Is he okay?" she demanded.

"He's okay." He rubbed his hand over her back.

She pulled away. It was too painful.

"He's at a neighbor's house," Xander finally answered.

"Were there causalities?" Jaysa held her hands together. Her nails were bitten to the quick.

"Omar is in the hospital. I don't know how bad he is. They won't tell me since I'm not next of kin. I've notified his sister. She's there with him."

"You both need medical attention. I'll drive you to the hospital," Jaysa said.

"I don't want to go," Olivia said. Even though her body ached all over, leaving the house sounded like more than she could accomplish.

"You need to get checked out, Olivia." Xander said.

"No," she said with resolve. "I'll go in the morning."

"Jaysa, there is a medical unit outside. Please ask them to come in and check us out when they're done." Xander reached for Olivia's right arm to help her off the floor.

The squeal she released rang throughout the house as she dropped back to the floor.

"Bae, that's it. I'm taking you to the hospital."

When she tried to resist, he picked her up gently and carried her out of the house.

"I'll work with Danny to put the house back in order," Jaysa said.

"I can walk, Xander." Olivia squirmed until he placed her feet on the ground. The street was cluttered with police cars and people milling around taking pictures. Xander blocked her view of the side of the house. The pain in her arm was too agonizing to object. "Where are we going?"

"I parked my truck up the hill. We'll pick up Luc on the way."

She nodded and allowed him to tuck her into the curve of his body. She rested against him as they made their way. Each step gave pain free access to her body, radiating from one limb to the next. She just wanted the day to fade into tomorrow.

The moment Xander stepped foot on Margaret's porch, the door opened. "He hasn't stopped crying since he woke up."

Luc pushed past Margaret and charged at Xander's legs.

"Is everything okay at your place?" Margaret asked.

"It is now." He scooped up Luc. "I'll explain later. Thanks for looking after Luc."

At the hospital, Olivia laid on a cot while Luc sat on Xander's lap next to the bed. It didn't take long for the doctor to walk back into the room with a handful of paper.

"Olivia, I have your x-rays. You've torn your rotator cuff," he said while flipping through the papers. "You can do physical therapy, but PT will just prolong the inevitable. Eventually, you're going to need surgery to repair the tear. And if you wait too long, it will be like trying to stitch together fish scales," the doctor grimaced. "I'll have the nurse come in to get something scheduled."

"But it only hurts when I do this," she tried to raise her hand above her head.

"Yeah, so stop doing that," he chuckled and turned to Xander. "We're going to change the dressing on your shoulder. Thankfully, it's just a flesh wound. You should be fine in a couple of days."

When the doctor walked out, Olivia shook her head. How could bad things keep coming? There had to be an end.

"I failed you," she said to Xander when they were on their way home. "I had a shot. A good one. A kill shot and I couldn't do it. That's when he came after me and yanked my arm so hard, he must have torn the tendon."

Xander stared straight ahead. His eyes were locked on the road, but his jaw moved back and forth.

"Did you hear me?"

"Bae, killing someone is supposed to be hard. You're alive and so is Jaysa. You must have done something right."

She grabbed the sides of her head. "If we're going to get married, I need to be able to protect myself."

"Are you afraid? Do you think every job I take will be like this one?" He took his eyes off the road to glance at her.

"Err…" She couldn't lie to him, but she knew how he would respond. He'd say he would protect her. It was his job. But that wasn't good enough for her. Not since Ajay spent close to a year terrorizing her. Never again did she want to be that helpless and that dependent on someone else to fix her problem.

"You don't think I can keep you safe?"

"It's not your job."

"That's exactly what my job is. People pay me millions to keep them, their property, and their operations safe. But you don't think I can do that for you?"

The agony in his words filled the car. And she knew she'd been the one to put it there. After everything she'd been through today, this wasn't the conversation they needed to have. Not now.

She glanced in the back seat at Luc. His big eyes were filled with fear as he sucked his thumb. "Can we talk about this later?"

CHAPTER 35

X ander sat on one end of the sofa and Jimmie on the other. The tightness of the police chief's face said he wanted answers and he wasn't willing to wait.

"So, you're telling me you killed five men today. What the hell do you think this is? You're not some swashbuckling mercenary. You can't take the law into your hands and run things the way you see fit. The prime minister has been calling me every few hours. The body count keeps going up and I have no explanations. Do you have any idea what this can do to our tourist trade?" He shook his head. "I'm not happy, Xander. Not at all." The anger in Jimmie's voice echoed through every room of the house.

"I didn't bring this element to Sebastian. You can thank Kais Bisset for that, and the last I heard, he was good friends with the prime minister."

"This is not the time to joke. I usually let you do your thing, but someone has got to answer for the destruction that took place out at that shack."

Xander tried to ignore his throbbing head. This wasn't

the conversation he wanted to have this evening. He'd rather be curled in bed with Olivia and Luc watching a Disney movie and listening to Luc laugh. Like old times. That had been the plan until hell came knocking. "What would you do, Jimmie? Luc was in my care. He lost his father. You would have done the same thing. You would have turned the world upside down to find someone you cared about."

"Well, that's what you did... Turned our peaceful island upside down." He pushed to the edge of his seat. "Charges may be filed against you and your company. Get a good lawyer."

"That is the last thing I'm worried about. Don't you want to know why this guy—Lawrence went through so much trouble for paintings that are forged, fakes? Why they kidnapped that little boy? Why Eliza is missing?"

Jimmie pounded his fist on the sofa arm. "I don't give a damn. What I want you to do is call the police and let us do our job. That shack was on our radar. We would have checked it out."

"When? How long would Luc have had to wait for you and your team to get there?" Xander's voice rose too and he regretted his words. "I'm sorry, Jimmie. I know your guys were working on it, but I couldn't wait."

Jimmie stood and pulled his khaki shorts higher on his waist. "Then be prepared for what happens next. This may be something I can't protect you from. And please, no more dead bodies. This isn't New York, our morgue isn't that big."

Xander nodded. "As long as no one comes after me and my family, I won't pull out my gun."

"Very funny. You look like shit. Get some sleep and say hello to a razor. I'll let myself out." Jimmie shoved his pad in his pocket and walked out.

Xander remained on the sofa and waited for the quiet to soothe his injured ego. The discussion with Jimmie wasn't as threatening as the things Olivia had said. No matter what he thought he could do, if Olivia didn't feel safe, then it meant nothing. And maybe she was half right. She and Luc weren't killed, but they were hurt. He shrugged his wounded shoulder as the stiffness took over. Everyone in the house had been injured one way or another. He would be okay and so would Olivia, but Luc concerned him. He was too young to articulate his emotions and he'd been through so much in the last few days.

Xander called the hospital and the only information they provided for Omar was no change. Omar had suffered internal damage and lost a lot of blood. Until Xander knew Omar was going to be okay, focusing on anything was almost impossible.

At least by the time they'd returned home from the hospital, the police cars and emergency vehicles were gone. Jaysa had even hired a crew to straighten up the inside. The broken glass was gone and the furniture was back in place.

He picked up the phone and bellowed. "Danny, what happened to the crew that was supposed to be watching my house? How did Lawrence get men inside my place?"

"You called them and asked them to back up the mission at the shack."

"I did no such thing. If that's the story they want to go with, then their jobs are in jeopardy." Xander didn't try to hide his anger. Things at the house could have gone much worse.

"Xander, I heard the recording. It was you."

"It sounded like me, but I was in the woods with you. I had no time to make a call and if I did, I wouldn't have pulled them off this security detail. We have protocols for this."

"In the recording, you gave them the codes, Xander. I can't explain what's going on, but they were following orders that sounded like they came from you."

He closed his eyes. Danny's words rolled around in his head like loose marbles. "This doesn't make any sense. We'll regroup tomorrow. Whatever is going on, we need to get it straightened out. It impacts too many people."

After making plans to get the whole team together, Xander hung up.

The phone on his desk shook him from his thoughts. He charged across the room and grabbed it from the receiver before it disturbed Luc or Olivia.

"Xander, it's me, Mike. Sorry for checking in so late. All hell broke out here."

Xander rested his elbow on the desk, steadying himself. "Give me the details."

Mike paused for a moment too long. Something hadn't gone as planned he could tell by the way Mike hesitated. "We found Eliza."

"What did she say? Was she in on this chaos?"

"She's in the hospital, Xander. And according to the information I got from the hospital, she's pretty bad."

Xander sat up straighter. His chest tightened around Mike's words. "What happened?"

"I'm not sure of all the details, but she was beaten. When we rescued her, she was conscious and only a little bruised. But now the doctor says if she makes it through the night, it will be a miracle. Maybe there were internal injuries."

He dropped his forehead into the palm of his hand. "Was anyone else hurt?"

"We got a couple of wounds, but nothing we won't recover from. What we didn't get was any answers on this Lawrence character. If the people holding Eliza knew him, the ones that aren't dead, aren't talking."

Xander's shoulders sank. Exhaustion clawed at him, threatening to drag him into the dark abyss. He could handle tough—in this business he'd learned that early, but he hadn't calculated the toll it would take when people so close to him were this involved.

"Mike, I'll check in with you in the morning. Make sure Eliza has protection… just in case." He placed the phone back on the receiver and pushed away from the desk. Before he left the office, the phone rang again. "Yeah," he said without checking the caller ID.

"Mr. Fitzgerald, I've underestimated you. But let me warn you, don't assume I'm going away. I've paid for my painting and I intend to get what belongs to me."

"Lawrence, I've had a long day. Your guys kidnapped an innocent little boy, broke into my home, assaulted my fiancé, and walked out of here with the paintings. If you think I'm going to let you get away with that, I can assure you, we have unfinished business and now I'm mad. I don't like shitheads who beat up on women."

"Don't play games with me, Fitzgerald. First, Eliza comes to New York without my painting and now you claim, I've taken it. I don't know what game you're playing, but I'm far from amused. Until I get my painting, nobody you know is safe," Lawrence barked before hanging up.

Xander thumped the phone against his palm. He pinched the bridge of his nose. This whole thing was becoming more bizarre, and the only person who could provide answers was clinging to life. She needed to pull through; she had a son depending on her.

Without turning off any lights, he trudged to the opposite end of the house. At least this side of the house hadn't seen destruction like the other living spaces. Luc and Olivia were curled in the king-size bed. She had her arm draped over him as if she wanted to protect him. He shed his clothes down to his boxers and climbed in the bed beside Olivia. She'd said some hurtful things earlier, but he couldn't be mad at her. He placed his arm over her, protecting her the same way she protected Luc. She exhaled softly and backed into him. Having her in his arms was the best thing that had happened all day. She smelled like her favorite almond oil soap. He pressed his nose against her neck and inhaled her sweetness.

"I'm sorry about what I said earlier," she whispered. "I'm having a bad couple of days."

"We both are."

CHAPTER 36

By the time the sun spilled through the balcony doors, Olivia was ready to crawl out of bed. Sleeping sandwiched between Xander and Luc was comforting, but no matter how badly she wanted to stay there, her mind wouldn't stop racing. The events of the last two days were more traumatic than the stuff she'd gone through with Ajay.

She shifted her body until she was flat on her back. Xander's arm rested around her waist. He'd snored softly in her ear all night, exhaustion in every breath. What she needed now was to ease out of bed without disturbing Luc or Xander so she could have a minute alone with her thoughts. She lifted Xander's arm and inched her way to the foot of the bed. Once she stood, she glanced back at Xander and Luc. They looked so much alike–one small, one large. Many times, she'd wondered how so many people could see the two of them together and not notice the resemblance. She couldn't be the only one. Unless, once again, she was looking for ways to sabotage the best thing in her life. It wouldn't be the first time love scared her away. She thought things would be different with Xander, but the haunting fear that she hadn't changed faced her down. She just needed to know if she was strong enough and woman enough to fight for the love she deserved and wanted.

Her heart was so intertwined with Xander. The thought of not always having him by her side made her body ache even more. Nobody had ever loved or cared for her the way he did. But when she'd envisioned her happily-ever-after, it never included guns and assaults and torn tendons and kidnapping. She padded off to shower before the house was once again engulfed in a crush of people vying for answers and Xander's attention.

When she stepped back in the bedroom, Luc was sitting up in the bed rubbing his eyes. He spotted her and started toward her. She pointed toward Xander and held her index finger to her mouth for Luc to be quiet.

When they stepped out of the bedroom, she closed the door and bent to pick Luc up. She winced at the pain that shot through her shoulder but didn't release him. "What would you like for breakfast today?"

"I wanna go home." His sad voice tugged at the maternal instincts she didn't know she had. "I want Mommy."

"You don't want to leave us already, do you? We have so much fun stuff planned for you." She bounced him on her hip and walked toward the bedroom where his bags were stored. "How about we get you a bath and get dressed? Then you can help me cook breakfast for Xander."

He placed his head on her shoulder without a word, but she was certain he hadn't changed his mind about leaving.

The doctor had assured Xander that Luc hadn't suffered any physical injury while he was with his kidnappers, but as he sat at the kitchen counter watching Olivia pull the eggs and bacon from the refrigerator, he hadn't made a sound.

The happy glow that usually twinkled in his eyes when he sucked his thumb was missing.

Olivia cracked eggs into the bowl. "Let's play a game, Luc."

He nodded.

"I'll tell you what's making me sad today, and then you can tell me what's making you sad." She pushed the bowl of eggs aside and placed her elbows on the counter to be eye level with him.

"Okay." His voice was almost inaudible.

"I'm sad we didn't get to finish our day on the beach like we planned. I'm sad that man took you away from me." She pointed to her left eye and her lip. "I'm sad the skin around my eye is blue and my lip is still swollen, and I'm sad my shoulder hurts." She waited a moment as his eyes studied her face. "Now your turn."

"I'm sad because I miss my dad. I'm sad because my mom didn't call yesterday to tell me goodnight. I'm sad because I left Wooby at the beach, and I'm sad because I wasn't supposed to talk to strangers and I'm going to be in trouble."

She rushed around the counter and scooped him into her arms. "You are not in trouble, sweetheart," she whispered in his ear. "That man is the one in trouble. You did nothing wrong. And as for your giraffe, we'll get you a new one. That one was kinda old and dirty anyway. Okay?"

He nodded his head.

"I'm sure your mother wanted to call you last night. Maybe we missed her call when we were at the hospital about my arm. We'll try to reach her later today. Will that make you happy?" She pulled him away from her chest to see his face. The start of a smile tugged at his lips.

"Yes." He wiggled away from her and climbed off the stool. "Is Xander mad at me?"

"He could never be mad at you. You know that." Her

answer seemed to release all the trouble from his chest and his face brightened. If she had a little boy, she'd want him to be exactly like Luc. He was such a caring child. He didn't seem to notice how she skipped over the mention of his father. That was an area so raw and tender, she wasn't sure she could address it without both of them falling into tears. By now, either his mother should have called or Mike should have called with news of her. She glanced at the clock on the wall. After breakfast, she would contact Mike for an update.

Olivia turned back to Luc. "How about we start breakfast so the smell wakes Xander?"

Luc pointed to the remaining eggs beside the bowl. "Can I crack the eggs?" He'd climbed back on his stool and was reaching for the egg carton.

"Did I hear my name?" Xander moseyed into the kitchen. Even with a bad case of bed-hair, he was still the most attractive man she'd ever seen. The two of them wore bruises from the previous days, but nothing lessened the way her heart sped up every time she looked at him.

"We're making you breakfast," Luc chirped while dropping an egg and shell into the bowl.

"Yes, and you had better hurry up and get dressed. We've got a big day planned." Olivia fished the shell out of the bowl. While she and Luc might be in a good mood, it was obvious that Xander's thoughts weren't as jovial. He leveled a look at Olivia that settled in her stomach like a heavy weight. She couldn't interpret what was going on, but since going to bed last night, something else bad had happened.

CHAPTER 37

Xander stood under the hot spray of the shower and allowed the water to rinse the soap from his body. He hoped the warmth would loosen the tension and aches in his body. Today wasn't going to be easy. Bad news continued breaking, and nothing had been settled yet. Lawrence was looking for his painting. Eliza and Omar were hospitalized. Olivia needed surgery. He might be facing charges, and a whole host of other things were waiting to take a bite out of his ass.

He pressed his forehead against the cold marble and took several deep breaths. He needed to untangle the web and find the small clues that had been overlooked.

From the bedroom, the chatter of Olivia and Luc reached him and lightened his mood. At least they'd found something to make them laugh. Olivia was the woman he wanted to make a life and start a family with. But he couldn't make her feel comfortable with a future together. She had to find her way there alone. All he could do was what he did best—protect her and keep her safe. Show her.

He took his time dressing. Sometime this morning

he'd have to tell Olivia about Eliza's condition. Telling Luc would be the hardest task. He'd lost his father, and now his mother was close to death. The little boy probably had no idea what any of it meant. At four-years-old, he had no idea how all this was going to impact him.

Xander strolled into the kitchen to the smell of crisp bacon. His stomach churned. He hadn't eaten in over twenty-four hours. How was that even possible?

"Just in time." Olivia placed the platter of eggs, bacon, and biscuits in the center of the table.

"I helped with breakfast." Luc had his knees in the chair leaning over the food with his fork. "I rolled this one right there." He pointed to an oddly shaped biscuit that looked like a half moon.

He smiled at Luc and reached for the platter, raking a pile of food onto his plate. "What's on the agenda today?"

"We're gonna get me a new wooby. I left my other one on the beach. Olivia promised."

Olivia kissed the top of Luc's head and took a seat at the table. "How about a nice quiet day with no major disruptions?"

"If I could order up one of those, I certainly would." Xander chewed a piece of bacon.

Olivia looked at him across the table. "After breakfast, I'm going to give Mike a call to see how they made out yesterday." She was being careful not to use Eliza's name.

"I talked with him last night." Xander glanced at Luc who was busy smearing jelly onto his special-made biscuit.

"Who's Mike?" Luc asked without looking up.

"Someone who works for me, buddy." Xander mussed Luc's hair, then leveled his eyes on Olivia.

Without having to say anything, she registered his message. Now was not the time to talk about Eliza. Olivia's eyes dropped to her plate. She pushed the eggs from one side of the plate to the other without taking a bite.

Xander lifted his head and mustered some cheerfulness. "I've got to debrief with the team this morning. Why don't the three of us ride over to the facility? I shouldn't be there too long. Afterwards, we can get some ice cream and a new toy for you, Luc."

Luc beamed, but Olivia's face said she wasn't fooled. "You want us to go with you?"

"Yeah," he shrugged his shoulder. "I won't be long."

Olivia stood and moved her plate to the sink. She dumped the eggs into the garbage disposal without looking at him. "Luc, go put on your shoes so we can get ready to go."

The boy bounded off the chair and out of the kitchen.

"You want to tell me what's going on?" She came to stand between his legs and cupped her hands around his face. "You've never invited me to the center before."

Xander pulled her closer. "I don't want you and Luc out of my sight."

"Do you think we're in danger?"

"I don't know. But if you're with me, I'll feel better."

"You know the three of us can't be together all the time. It's not possible."

"This isn't forever. It's just for now. Humor me for a couple of days. Okay?"

"Okay," she said. "And what did Mike say last night when you talked with him?"

He didn't answer right away. It was hard enough thinking Eliza might not pull through, putting it into words was ten times harder.

"Tell me, Xander," she demanded.

"She was beaten. Pretty bad. The doctors said it would be a miracle if she made it through the night." The words sounded foreign coming out of his mouth. No matter how many times he said it, there was a ring of unfamiliarity about it all.

Olivia placed her head in his lap. Even without seeing her face, he knew she was crying. Her shoulders shook. "Oh my, God. How will you tell Luc?"

"I don't know yet. I'm going to wait as long as I can. Hopefully, there won't be anything to tell." He pulled her to her knees and covered her mouth with his. The sweet smell of her skin and the softness of her mouth would get him through the day.

CHAPTER 38

Olivia buckled Luc into his car seat. Xander stood at the hatch of the car surveying their surroundings. He didn't say it, but she knew he was checking for unidentified cars or strangers in the neighborhood. Every muscle in his body was on high alert. She glanced around, not sure what she expected to see, and then climbed into the car.

If she could spend the day in her studio looking at pictures or taking photographs on the beach, the foreboding in her stomach might ease. But that kind of freedom and carefreeness was unavailable to her for now. Xander might have his confident stroll and air of preparedness, but the way he clenched his jaw said he had concerns also.

"How long do you think we'll have to live like this?" she whispered. It was a question she knew he didn't have an answer for, but she needed to ask. To float the idea out there, so he'd know her concern. She wanted their life back. The one where they could make love on the balcony without worrying about being watched. Where she could walk down the street and not worry about someone following her. Where she could play hide and seek with Luc on the beach and not worry that someone would steal him away.

Xander reached for her hand and gave it a squeeze. "It won't be long. Trust me." He turned the ignition and pulled out of their lane.

She bit her bottom lip.

"I know this is difficult for you, Olivia." There was a firmness in his voice that wasn't there earlier.

She rubbed his arm. "I do trust you. With all my heart, I do. I'm just nervous. What's happening here is not new for you. You're trained for this level of anxiety. Until Ajay lost his mind, I lived a calm life. The most exciting thing I did was ziplining on vacation in Virginia and that only lasted sixty seconds."

The tension in his face relaxed. "We're both in unfamiliar territory. My family has never been harmed before. This is more anxiety than I'm used to because you and Luc have been dragged into this case. Just be patient, this will be resolved soon."

Luc was so excited about shopping for his new toy, he chatted about it all the way to the facility. When Xander pulled the car into his spot in front of the building, Olivia realized she hadn't been paying much attention to the conversation. The idea of going inside was daunting. Two years on the island and she never had a reason to enter before. Even when Xander met her for lunch, he always waited outside when she arrived.

Xander came around and opened her car door before releasing Luc from his car seat. He wrapped one arm around her waist and held Luc's hand as he escorted them toward the entrance. His touch was the calming effect she needed as she walked through the door of the cave where he kept all his secrets. Luc released his hand and bounded ahead. For him, this was just another adventure to endure before toy shopping.

"Olivia, you're tense." Xander tightened his hand on her waist.

"Stop worrying about me. I'm fine."

The large facility was lit up like Times Square. Computers lined the wall and technical devices cluttered the table. Men seated at the large oval table looked up when Xander walked in.

"If you'll feel more comfortable, you can wait over there until I'm done." He pointed to a sofa that was angled in the corner.

"I want to know what's going on. The more I know, the better I can prepare for what's happening."

He inhaled. The skeptical expression on his face let her know he didn't think it was a good idea, but her mind was made up.

He settled Luc on the sofa and handed him a gaming tablet, and then led her toward his waiting team on the opposite side of the large room. "Okay, let's debrief." Xander sat in the only armchair at the table.

Danny cleared his throat. "Here's what we know." He glanced at his tablet. "There are two operations in play here. A cartel out of New Jersey and Lawrence Cistos. The cartel is into drugs, prostitution and gambling. I'm not sure what Lawrence's deal is. He has quite a reputation for being ruthless, but he doesn't have a criminal record and he avoids the press and social media. We found a picture of him, but it's dated twenty years ago. He hires out all of his dirty work."

"We're dealing with both of them?" A vein in Xander's neck bulged.

"Thanks to Calvin and Jeffrey, we are now. The two of them were trying to run a little side drug hustle, skimming from the cartel. I don't think Calvin knew how deep the operation went. He might have thought Jeffrey was operating on his own."

"Until he got shot," Xander said. "So, let me lay this out. Lawrence wants a painting. That's all he wanted or ever wanted. Jeffrey and Calvin compromised everything when they crossed the cartel."

"Well, almost. It looks like Kais Bisset crossed Lawrence when he decided he could get a better price for the artwork. That started the catastrophic events." Danny tapped a few screens on his tablet.

Olivia sat up straighter before addressing the team. "How does Eliza play into all of this?"

"Well, we know she was involved with Jeffrey. She knew about his drug business. But I don't think she knew anything about the hit at the storage unit or the kidnapping or her husband's murder. I'm still digging," Danny said.

Olivia tried to absorb the information, but the level of deceit and deception was beyond her understanding. She was a photographer. Looking at life through a lens laid everything out in the open. Photoshopping was the closest she came to altering reality. Eliza was a mother and respected in the community. She had a fabulous life. Why was she willing to throw it all away?

Xander nodded. "It's starting to make sense now. Those boxes stolen from the storage unit—drugs, right?"

"Affirmative," Danny answered.

"How did the watch on my house get cancelled?" Xander tapped his fingers on the table.

"That was Calvin again. We were able to trace his activity on our computers. Last week, he logged into the system and got the codes. Once he had that, we think he spliced together a recording using your voice. He must have given it to someone or several people. We don't know if he was forced to do that, but he could have talked to someone. We have several communication processes in place for this kind of thing."

"We'll need to revamp. There may be other sensitive information that Calvin passed along," Xander proclaimed.

Olivia pushed away from the table. She'd heard enough. Her body craved air that wasn't polluted with betrayal. She locked eyes with Xander. "I'm going to keep Luc company on the sofa."

CHAPTER 39

Somewhere in the house, Xander heard Olivia and Luc building a dinosaur using the new set of connecting blocks they'd bought the day before. Leaving his office to join them would have been more enjoyable than threading through pages and pages of computer data. But as long as Luc could laugh, then he'd claim a small victory.

His cell phone vibrated, and he reached for it without screening the call. It had become useless trying to determine who to talk to and who to ignore. Every time the phone rang, it could be news on Eliza or Lawrence with another empty threat.

"Xander Fitzgerald, please. This is Standard Labs."

He gripped the phone tighter. In all the confusion, he'd been waiting for and dreading this call. He'd accepted Luc as his son the moment Olivia said the words aloud. Now, if it turned out he was wrong, it would be another crushing blow to place on the pile with all the others.

"Yeah, this is Xander."

"Can you verify your date of birth?"

He provided the date and waited.

"I've got the results from the paternity test. You wanted us to call you as soon as we got the results." The woman's crisp voice was no-nonsense. Xander appreciated her professionalism. If she had wanted to chat him up with talk about the humidity or the upcoming Bongo Festival, he would have vented his frustration. "The results say there is a 99.8% chance that Luc Bisset is your son. We've got the documentation and will courier it to the address provided." She paused long enough to take a breath. "Do you have any questions?"

He shook his head, then realized she couldn't see him or the wide grin that had taken over his face. "No. I'm good." He ended the call. His body felt like it was levitating out of the chair. He pushed air out of his mouth and soaked in the goodness of the news. He was Luc's father. He closed his eyes to the spinning room. When he opened them, he pounded his fist on the table. "My son," he whispered.

In the living room surrounded by a mountain of blue, green, red and yellow blocks, Olivia and Luc had their heads pressed together chewing jellybeans.

"I thought you two were building a dinosaur?" Xander sat crossed-legged in front of them and shoved his phone into his pocket.

"We decided to have a snack." Luc popped a green jellybean in his mouth and handed Xander a black one. He accepted the jellybean and popped it in his mouth.

"You've got the brightest smile on your face right now. Something good must have happened." Olivia rocked forward and planted her palms on his knees. "What is it?"

"I got news." He couldn't take his eyes off Olivia. When he gave her the news, he wanted to read the expression on her face and in her eyes. Forget what she might say, he wanted to see how she felt.

"Are you going to tell me or are you just going to grin for the rest of the day?"

"I just got a call from Standard Labs. You were right." He had to talk in code. Even though Luc seemed to be absorbed in his toys and the candy, he managed to hear everything.

Olivia squealed. Her eyes flashed with unmistakable joy. The joy on her face infiltrated his heart and it was as if he'd fallen in love with her again. She came up on her knees and wrapped an arm around his neck. "That's so great." She swayed her body back and forth, which made him lose his balance and the two of them tumbled to the floor.

"Are we playing a new game?" Luc asked.

"Yeah, we are." Olivia made room for Luc, who piled into them. The three of them giggled and laughed and tickled each other until Luc grew tired and returned to his blocks leaving Xander alone with Olivia.

"You sure you're okay with this?" he asked.

She put her index finger to his lips. "How can you even ask me a question like that? If it weren't for me, you'd still be in a state of denial. The question, now that you know, should be are you okay?"

He couldn't take his eyes off her face. Everything she said and did in these moments needed to be remembered. If he missed a sigh or a moment when she looked away, he needed to know. The news that Luc was his son was too important to miss the smallest detail of how it might impact his life with Olivia. Everything she said and did right now mattered.

"You know, the last few days, I've tried not to think about the results. I was afraid the answer might come back telling me I wasn't. So, I didn't allow myself to get too wrapped up in the idea. At least not aloud, only in my head." He tapped his temple. "But now that I know for sure, I can't explain how complete I am." He pulled her down on top of him again. "I have you. I have him," he whispered, nodding toward Luc. "My life is damn near perfect."

"What would make it perfect?" She seemed to pulse with excitement.

"You, Bae. When I can call you my wife." It was a thought he'd had several times a day over the last months, and he'd said it to her almost as often. But it was a realization she had to come to on her own. After today, he wouldn't mention marriage again.

Her warm brown eyes sparkled. She reached out and ran her finger along his jawline. "I have to marry you now, so you won't be a single parent." She chuckled when he embraced her in another bear hug.

If she stayed by his side, he had a million reasons to be happy. He had to believe she'd get there if he was patient.

"Your phone is vibrating." Olivia pulled away and pointed at his pocket.

He fished it out and held it up. "Is it mean of me to wonder when was the last time I had a vacation right now?" He answered without screening. "Yeah."

"It's me, Mike. You need to come to New York as soon as possible."

Xander sat up straighter. "What's wrong?"

"It's Eliza. She might not make it through the night. She wants to see Luc."

"How much time do I have?"

"Get here today." There was no negotiating in Mike's voice. He wasn't a big man, but he spoke with authority. "I'll call Jaysa and have her arrange for a private plane. It should be ready for takeoff in two hours. Be there."

CHAPTER 40

Olivia stared out the window of the plane as it taxied toward the terminal at Teterboro Airport in New Jersey. The flight from Sebastian had been a quiet one. Luc fell asleep before they took off, and during the flight, Xander rubbed his chin so much she expected to see a smooth spot on his face before they made it to New York.

They had packed so fast, there wasn't any time to examine her feelings. Maybe not defining them was best because everything was fluid. There was no use settling on an idea that might change in the next few minutes.

"Olivia, did you hear me?" Xander asked.

"I'm sorry, sweetheart. What did you say?"

"A car will be waiting to take us straight to the hospital. Do you think we should tell Luc what's going on before we get there?"

Olivia reached across the aisle to run her fingers through Luc's hair. He'd fallen asleep with his head in Xander's lap. "How about we tell him we're taking him to see his mother. Maybe, Eliza will be able to tell him about her condition."

She shrugged her shoulders. "We don't know enough right now."

Xander gave her an eager nod. "You're right."

She'd never seen him look so apprehensive. Being a father was an added responsibility for him to carry. If only there was some way to assure him that he didn't have to do this alone. She'd help him sort it out. Together, they'd figure out how to handle whatever came next.

The plane stopped, and a few minutes later they deplaned and were rushed through customs and immigration before climbing into the waiting car.

"Where are we going?" Luc asked. His voice was still thick with sleep.

She gave Xander a quick glance and held her breath.

"We're taking you to see your mother." Xander looked down at Luc and said the words in such a reassuring way, she almost forgot how dire the situation might be at the hospital.

"My mom?" Luc bounced in the seat. "Am I going to stay with her now?"

"We'll see, buddy." Xander lifted his head, stared straight ahead and started rubbing his chin again.

She had as much anxiety as he did. She just hid hers on the inside, but the sandwiches they'd picked up on the way to the plane threatened to come back up at any minute.

When the car pulled up to Mount Sinai Hospital in Manhattan, Luc never registered the significance of them going into a hospital.

Mike met them at the entrance. "You guys made good time."

"We had to, right?" Xander replied. "Has there been any change?"

Olivia watched as he held his breath and waited for the answer.

"Yes. Now let's go." Mike led the way to the bank of elevators.

Xander worried for Luc's sake. He'd done everything possible to get him to the hospital in time to see his mother. Olivia focused on the elevator panel, and as the numbers climbed so did her heart rate. Not knowing how the night would end rattled her nerves more than the flight to New Jersey. She patted Xander on the leg as she groped for his hand. He grabbed it and gave her a reassuring squeeze.

"Have you seen Eliza?" Olivia asked Mike.

"No, I'm not allowed in the room. The police are guarding her door and only a few officials have been inside."

"Don't you think a policeman standing outside her door might be upsetting to Luc?" Olivia spoke out of the side of her mouth as low as she could so Luc wouldn't hear.

"I'll go ahead of you guys and excuse the guard until Luc's inside the room."

The elevator doors parted, and Mike stepped off and disappeared around the corner ahead of them the way they'd planned. Olivia had to hold on tight to Luc's hand because he wanted to go charging to his mother. "Wait a minute, Luc," she said.

Xander got the signal on his phone, and the three of them made their way to Eliza's room. Olivia stayed back and allowed Xander and Luc to go inside. She wrung her hands and walked a small circle a few feet from the room. Within seconds, Xander came out without Luc.

She rushed to his side. "What happened?"

"She wanted time alone with Luc." Xander turned to Mike. "You said she wouldn't make it through the night. She doesn't look sick to me. I expected to see a ventilator and all kinds of monitors and plugs. Other the the IV, there is nothing."

Mike held up his hands. "I repeated what I was told. I haven't seen her or talked to her doctors."

Xander hooked his thumbs through his beltloops. "Something's not making sense." He scratched his head. "After the events of the last few days, I shouldn't be surprised."

"Nobody is telling me anything. I'm following orders around here." Mike snapped back.

The tension must be getting to all of them. Olivia shot the two of them a firm stare. "Shhh, I don't want Luc to hear us arguing. He's been through enough."

Xander moved to her side and draped an arm across her shoulders. The moment he pulled her close, the tension seemed to leave his body. Together, they were perfect. He always provided the assurances she needed, and she steadied him when his work was overwhelming. With a flow this natural, marriage was the logical next step, but she wasn't ready to take it. His work was dangerous. Marrying him was like marrying a police officer. Every time he accepted a new case, she'd worry how it might impact their lives. There was always the potential he wouldn't come home or he'd come home different—physically or mentally.

"There is a waiting room at the end of the hall." Mike pointed in the direction they'd come.

"I'd rather wait here for Luc when he comes out." Xander turned to face Eliza's room.

After almost an hour, Luc walked out of the room. Big tears hung from his thick lashes. Xander dropped to his knees in front of Luc, and Olivia's heart constricted at the sight. Xander was ready to be a father. He deserved to be a father, and she was the one holding him back from his dream family. Her indecisiveness about marriage was enough to tear them apart, but moving forward was just as fearful.

"Are you okay?" Xander cushioned Luc's cheeks between his palms and stared into his eyes.

Luc gave Xander a slow nod. "She wants to see you and Olivia."

Olivia pressed her hand to her throat, unsure she'd heard what Luc said. She wanted Eliza to recover and for all of their lives to return to normal, but the two of them hadn't said more than a few words to each other since the big party at the Bisset house, which now seemed like eons ago. "Your mom wants to see me too?"

Luc nodded.

She caught the concern in Xander's eyes. "Did she say why?" Xander asked.

This time Luc shrugged his shoulders. For a little boy, he had been through too much. Xander pulled Luc into his chest and hugged him close, then he turned to Mike. "Can you take Luc down to the waiting room? After we're done, Olivia and I will come down there."

Mike stuck out his hand and Luc grabbed his fingers. The two of them made their way down the sterile corridor. Luc's head bent to the floor, making Mike appear even taller walking alongside him.

"Why do you think Eliza wants to see me?" Olivia's heart thumped in her chest.

"I have no idea. When it comes to Eliza, we need to go in there and be prepared for anything. I hope she's ready to tell the truth and fill in the remaining blanks." Xander held her hand and applied enough pressure to give her some assurance that the two of them would handle whatever awaited them on the other side of Eliza's door.

CHAPTER 41

Xander led Olivia toward Eliza's room without releasing her hand. The antiseptic smell and the eerie quiet of the hospital loomed over him like a foreboding cloud. Nothing good ever came from a hospital visit unless someone was having a baby. And Olivia wasn't pregnant.

He and Olivia were going to see this through to the end, together. Whatever Eliza said or did wouldn't matter if Olivia remained by his side. She was the love he had been looking for even before he'd known he needed her.

The walk to Eliza's door was only a few feet, but it seemed much longer. His stomach was uneasy, but all his dealings with Eliza had been turbulent. Fraught with mistrust, misinformation, and misunderstandings. With all her beauty and wealth, Eliza was a troubled woman at her core.

Olivia hesitated. "Maybe you should go in there alone." The worry lines on her forehead deepened as she stalled and tried to let go of his hand.

"Bae, we're going to do this together. Whatever Eliza tells

us—me, I want you to hear it too." Without releasing her hand, he continued toward the door tugging Olivia along instead of them easing into it together.

At the door, he paused for an instant, then walked inside. Eliza sat up in the bed, her eyes were red and puffy. The abrasions on her face were the only indication that she'd suffered any trauma. Someone had used her face for a punching bag. She glanced at them, then pressed a tissue to her nose and blew. Eliza had never appeared more vulnerable. Without her customary lush surroundings, her looming presence was minimized. Olivia tucked her shoulders back and stayed by his side.

"How are you, Eliza?" She stopped at the foot of the bed and put her hands together.

Eliza cleared her throat.

"Are you going to tell us what's going on?" Xander's patience had waned. He needed answers. This wasn't a social call. It was obvious that Eliza wasn't near death, so the late-night flight to New York was another hoax.

Eliza held up her hand, and Olivia gave him a look that demanded he let things progress at Eliza's pace.

"Luc misses you. Every day he asks when he is going to talk to his mom." Olivia's tone was consoling. Of course, she wanted to take a gentler approach. A sledgehammer wasn't big enough for how he wanted to obliterate this whole mess.

Eliza took an exaggerated breath. "Did you take the paternity test?" She glared at him while rubbing her thumb along her index finger.

"He's my son." There was no emotion in his voice.

She nodded back and forth, rocking her upper body. "Yeah, I know."

Xander bit back his anger percolating below the surface. "You wasted four years."

"Look, I'm just going to say what I need to say. I might as

well get this over." She huffed again. "I've cleared what I'm saying to you with the Feds."

Xander stepped closer to the bed. "The Feds? What have they got to do with this?"

"Let me tell this at my pace." She focused her attention on Olivia. "I want you and Xander to take Luc for me." She sniffed. It was almost as if saying those words caused her pain. "I'm going to be in the States for a few years. I'm going to testify against the Marcos Cartel. The Feds have promised to protect me until after the trial which won't begin until next year."

"So that's why they're saying you're dying?" Xander asked.

She nodded. "Yes, if the cartel thinks I'm dead, then maybe I'll be safer. At least until the trial gets closer."

"Are you going into witness protection?" Olivia came around the bed to stand next to him.

"Yeah. After the trial." Eliza stared at her feet that made two humps from under the sheet. "I've told Luc we won't see each other for a very long time, and he was going to live with you two. I know you both love him and will take care of my baby. Please don't let him forget me." She sniffed.

Her words tugged on his heart. "Wait a minute, Eliza." He shook his head. "This is moving too fast. There has got to be another way to handle this."

"There isn't, Xander. They almost killed me. Jeffrey double-crossed the Marcos family and they won't rest until they get their money back."

Olivia laid her hand on his shoulder. She was the diplomat, waiting while Eliza doled out details at her own pace. All he wanted to do was yank the information out of her throat.

"I thought I was helping him. I had no idea he was tied into a big drug cartel."

"You were having an affair with him?" Xander said.

"I loved him, Xander, and he loved me." She barked at him.

"What about Kais? Did you love him too? Did he know?"

"What about Kais? He didn't know and if he did, he wouldn't have cared. We didn't have that fairytale relationship like you and Olivia. We lived two separate lives. The only thing that held us together was Luc. I loved Kais, but I was never in love with him. And don't get sappy over our relationship. What we had worked for Kais, too. He had access to my money, and he was happy until he burned through the accounts."

"Who killed Kais?"

"I don't know." She said each word with emphasis. "I really don't know. I had nothing to do with it. You believe me, don't you?" Her eyes widened and she looked from him to Olivia.

"Yes," he answered slowly. "Yes, but it's hard to know what to believe. How do the paintings figure into all of this?"

Eliza closed her eyes, then opened them. He watched as she inhaled and exhaled through her mouth. There was no way of knowing if she was going to tell an elaborate lie or a partial truth.

"I overheard Kais talking on the phone one evening about the paintings. The bigger one was a decoy. Underneath was an original Renoir that was stolen from some gallery in Paris. When Kais found out, he started looking for someone who was willing to pay triple the price of the original buyer in New York." She rolled her thumb over her index finger again. "I mentioned it to Jeffrey. We thought we could use that painting to pay back the money Jeffrey owed the cartel, but they killed him. Then they started threatening me. They thought the painting was in the storage unit. So did I. When that shop owner called and told me the paintings were in her vault, I had to come to New York to try to negotiate with

Lawrence. To get the money. But he immediately knew the painting I brought with me wasn't the right one." She threw up her hands. "I don't know why I thought I could get away with something like that, but I had no choice. Kais and I are nearly broke. I was hoping to sell the Renoir and pay off Jeffery's debt. Then maybe I could save the house and live off the rest." She shook her head. "Nothing turned out the way I planned. If I don't help the Feds, I'm never going to be safe and neither is Luc."

"So, the cartel has the painting now and Lawrence is pissed as fuck," Xander said.

A stream of tears ran down Eliza's face.

Xander dropped his head and pinched the bridge of his nose so hard his sinuses stung.

CHAPTER 42

Eliza's hospital room was warm, and the temperature crept up one agonizing degree at a time. Olivia tried to keep her face neutral, but Eliza's revelation made it hard. Every nerve in her body was tuned into Xander, the way he breathed, the way he walked, the way he clenched his jaw. He never talked about his relationship with Eliza, but it couldn't have been an easy one. Even now, there was a current between them that would scorch anyone who came in contact with it.

"Are you sure you want us to take Luc?" Olivia had to push the words around the lump in her throat.

"I know it's a lot to ask, but Xander is his father." The knowing look Eliza gave her was a common language that only two women who loved the same man could understand. The expression on Xander's face was full of emotion. He looked like he was holding his breath, afraid to engage his hope because Eliza might snatch the coveted offer away just as quickly as she'd given it.

"For how long?" Olivia asked.

Even though Eliza sounded sure about her decision, the

facts, the details, needed more discussion. Xander needed protecting. His emotions were too exposed.

"It may be until he's of legal age. I've had the papers drawn up. Unfortunately, I don't have a lot of money to help with his care, but…"

"Wait a minute." Xander held his hand up. "What are you saying, Eliza? You're turning Luc's care over to us?" He glanced at Olivia.

Eliza focused on a fold in the blanket covering the bed. She teased the fabric. "I could take him into the protection program with me, but I think it's better if as much as possible stays normal for him. He gets to stay on the island. You can take him to the States to visit my parents and his cousins, and I know you love him. And you too, Olivia."

Olivia picked up Eliza's hand. She crushed it in an embrace to convey the enormity of the moment. "I love Luc. We both do." She glanced over her shoulder at Xander. "But this is drastic. Maybe there is another way, so you won't have to erase Luc from your life."

Xander moved forward. "Yes, give me some time. I'm sure I can come up with something."

Eliza extracted her hand from Olivia's. "Please don't make this harder than it already is. I've done nothing but think about this for hours. If there was any way for me to get out of this mess without giving up my son, I would have taken it. The only thing that makes this easier is knowing he will be with his father."

"How soon—"

"Tonight." Eliza reached into the side table and removed a stack of paper. "I've signed everything, and had it notarized. There is only about three hundred thousand dollars left in my account, but that goes to you, too."

"I don't want your money, Eliza. What about Luc? Hasn't he been through enough?"

"I am thinking about Luc," she yelled. "He's the only one I'm thinking about. I can't stop thinking about my precious baby."

The room fell silent. Olivia's heart raced in her chest. Everything was happening fast. There had to be something to say for moments like this, but Olivia couldn't pull it up. Eliza was asking them to take her son, to raise him for her. Of course, they would. But this moment was so intense, words were inadequate. The way her emotions fired, there was no way she'd pinpoint the right words. She and Xander were still trying to map out their life and now they'd have to include Luc. Eliza was so composed. It was hard to believe she was making such a momentous decision.

"You've given this a lot of thought. I can't think of anything I'd love more than to have Luc live with me. It's something I could have never imagined, especially like this… under these circumstances," Xander paused. "You know this is permanent? You may never see Luc again."

"I'll see him again. He might not see me, but I'll see him," Eliza said with certainty.

She held out both of her hands toward them. The three of them held hands, and Eliza said, "Take care of my baby. Don't let him forget me and only tell him about my good parts. Now, if you'll excuse me. I'm really exhausted." She released their hands, scooted down in the bed and pulled the blanket to her chin.

Eliza looked small and vulnerable. All the ill feelings evaporated. Any woman who could put the welfare of her child above her love for him garnered a place in Olivia's heart above all else. The bravery displayed by Eliza would forever change her standing.

Before exiting the room, Olivia bent over and placed a kiss on Eliza's cheek. "Don't worry about him. Luc is loved, and we'll make sure he knows that every day." She wanted to wipe away the tears streaming from Eliza's eyes, but she didn't dare do anything that personal.

"I'll be right out, Olivia," Xander said to her. Olivia nodded and hurried from the room. On the other side of the door, she leaned against the wall and gulped air that wasn't contaminated with hopelessness as tears streamed down her face, too.

With her eyes closed, she tried to envision what would happen later tonight and tomorrow and the next day. For them to settle into an everyday routine seemed impossible. It was going to take more than pancakes to make them a family.

CHAPTER 43

Xander stepped out of the car and stretched his hands over his head. There was comfort in being back on Sebastian Island. After the whirlwind trip to New York and the shift in the plates that balanced his world, the humidity and heat of the island was welcomed. Olivia was unusually quiet. This beautiful, bold woman always had something to say and seldom held back her opinion. There was only one way to interpret her silence and that sat on his chest like a boulder. She never even asked what he said when he stayed behind to talk to Eliza. It hadn't been much. He'd thanked her and kissed her bruised mouth.

Xander carried Luc into the house. After leaving the hospital, he'd cried himself to sleep. The last couple of days had been harder on him than anyone else. The world that he knew was now upside down. He had a whole new life to learn, and it was too much for a four-year-old to grapple with. Nobody understood that better than Xander. Even though Eliza had cleared the deck on the questions regarding this case, there was still a big gap. Who had the painting, now? Had Cistos gone after the cartel to get it back?

"Let me put Luc to bed." Xander used his foot to close the door. "Then we need to talk."

"Yeah," Olivia said as she made her way into the kitchen. A moment later, he heard the refrigerator open.

He pulled off Luc's shoes and started on his clothes. Handling him was like trying to shove gelatin through a straw. As soon as he got one leg out of his shorts, Luc flipped over. When he managed to get his arms out of his shirt, Luc curled into a ball. Xander sat on the edge of the bed and rubbed his face in the palms of his hands. He wasn't ready to be a full-time dad. What did he know about raising children—bedtimes, proper nutrition, chores, homework, playdates?

He pulled his head up. Thinking too much about the future never worked. Life had never given him a script of what was coming next, so this was no different. If Olivia wanted out, he'd have to let her go. But she needed to decide soon. If she wasn't going to stick around, it was time for her to make her exit. He had to think about Luc. His son didn't need any more major disruptions in his life. Xander wanted stability for Luc, and he certainly had enough love to give him.

Luc whimpered in his sleep, drawing Xander's attention. Luc's hair was tousled and there was a smudge on his cheek. The chocolate Mike had plied him with to keep him from crying in the waiting room, no doubt. Xander popped his thumb in his mouth, wet it and wiped at his son's face until the chocolate disappeared. Then with the deftness of a seasoned parent, he removed the t-shirt. With a satisfied smile, he closed the bedroom door.

Olivia wasn't in the kitchen where he'd last seen her. He made his way toward the master suite. A sliver of light peeked from under the door. Outside the door, he drew in a big breath. This next part wasn't going to be easy. But the day had been filled with difficult tasks. He needed to get them all out of the way.

He opened the door. Olivia was seated on the center of the bed in a see-through yellow nightie. Beside her was a tray containing a bottle of wine and two glasses. Her thick hair rested on her shoulders and framed her face in a mass of curls. Even with this much distance between them, he sensed the softness of her bronzed skin, knowing every curve of her body. He ached to touch and taste her. The warm smile that graced her face should have loosened the knot in his stomach, but nothing was going to do that.

"I thought we both could use a drink." Olivia held the bottle in the air. "I know the circumstances are far from ideal, but you're a father. A full-fledged father, that's reason enough to toast. Right?"

What he had to say could wait. He stripped down to his briefs without taking his eyes off her. "Yes." He crossed the room and climbed onto the bed beside her.

"So, you've unwound another mystery." She looked at him through her thick lashes.

"I can't take credit for this one. It solved itself. Eliza filled in the blanks. I was thinking the murder of Jeffrey and Calvin were related to Kais' death. But the two sinister deeds weren't related at all."

"Lawrence didn't get his paintings."

"If he wants them, he'll have to fight the Marcos Cartel." He dropped his head. "If only Kais and Eliza didn't have so many secrets, most of this could have been avoided. Maybe Eliza wouldn't have to disappear and abandon her son. Eliza owed Luc so much more than she gave him." He shook the disappointing thoughts away. "For tonight, I'm going to bask in the fact that I get to spend time with Luc and forget all the other stuff."

Olivia popped the cork and poured two glasses. They

clinked them together. "To parenthood," she said and took a sip.

He emptied more than half the glass, and then filled it again. He needed the courage the alcohol gave him.

She started to say something, but he held up his hand. "If you're going to talk about Eliza or her situation, don't. Not tonight. Let's just…find something happier to discuss."

"Okay," she repositioned her butt on the bed, "but tomorrow we need to think about raising a four-year-old."

"It's the only thing I've thought about since we left New Jersey. Schools, routines…" He shoved his fingers through his hair. "How do you feel about this, Olivia? Things are moving so fast."

"I love Luc, you know that. Now that you know he's your son… Under the circumstances, I can't imagine anything better than him being here with you all the time."

"But what about us? You've stalled on setting a date, which tells me you're reluctant. Now, I've got a son. If you were hesitant before, all I can imagine is that any minute now I'm going to see you fleeing down the road with the wind in your massive head of curls."

"Nothing has changed between us." She set her glass on the table beside the bed, then reached for the half-empty bottle of wine between them and removed it, too. She crawled onto his lap, straddling him, and encased him in an embrace that should have lifted his heart. Instead, it magnified the sadness of the moment. He had enough love to hold them together for a lifetime, but Olivia's carefree spirit needed space to flow and sway like the breeze coming in off the ocean.

When her mouth covered his, a warmth mixed with love and lust short-circuited his thinking as he accepted her tongue. The sweet taste of wine lingered in her mouth. Maybe he wanted too much—her and Luc. In his vision, they created a family. The mythical fairytale he'd given up on years ago when Hope shattered his heart.

He placed his arms around her waist and tightened his hold, as if he could keep her forever by force. Their tongues performed a slow rhythmic dance. One that they'd done so many times and yet it never grew old. He wanted to push away the prospect of what daylight might bring. As long as he held her, he could believe their lives would find a way to meld together in the happiness he envisioned for both of them.

But it was useless to fight reality. His brain could accept what his heart wouldn't. He pulled away from her and held her at arm's length.

"Olivia, I have to think about Luc. He's my responsibility now." A heaviness settled in the pit of his stomach.

Her eyes widened. Confusion puckered in the lines on her forehead. "*We* both have to think about Luc. What do you mean?"

He removed her from his lap and sat on the edge of the bed. She joined him. With his elbows resting on his thighs, he rubbed his hands together, preparing for the hardest thing he'd ever done.

CHAPTER 44

Olivia mimicked Xander's posture and positioned her elbows on her thighs. The stance gave her the side view of his face; it was enough to see he was wrestling with a burden. Her instinct fought over what to do, coax the words out of him or wait until he was ready to talk. In the course of a few hours, their lives had been threatened and then turned inside out. There were no answers for all the questions swirling in her head, but they would come. Living with Xander had taught her patience.

His breath became more rapid and the taut draw of his face unsettled her. Something was churning away at him, a little at a time. But from his posture, it threatened to pull him out to sea the same way the riptide had pulled Miles' grandson.

"What is it, Xander?" The moment she said the words, she wanted to retract them. Not knowing may have been better than the sinking sensation filling her stomach. Dread washed over her in a wave.

"I've got to think about Luc. He's only four and someone needs to put that little boy ahead of everything else in their life. I've got to be that someone." Xander was still beside her, but he was pulling away as if he were reeling in his love from her. Taking it back. Maybe he didn't think he had the capacity to love her and Luc. Relationships had ended before, although usually, it was a slow gradual process and by the time the bonds were severed, there was no emotional breakdown. But this time, her heart and soul were invested.

"Xander," she paused to gather her resolve. "What are you saying? Please just spit it out." The words tore at her throat. Inviting the hurt he needed to dish out was hard, but knowing he wanted out wouldn't make the not telling any easier.

"You know me, Olivia. I'm all in or I'm all out. I won't walk the middle line. Luc needs stability and I've got to provide that for him. If you decide in a month or two or a year from now, marrying me isn't what you want, we'll tear up his life again. I can't do that to him. Nor can I push you into marriage or motherhood," he stopped and pinched the bridge of his nose. The sound of him struggling to control his breathing only made the situation worse. If she could fix this, she would, but she was in a corner and couldn't claw her way out.

"You're right, Xander. Luc deserves better, but can't we take a little time to figure out what that is?"

He shook his head and pushed off the bed. "No." From across the room, he positioned his hands on the dresser. "I was willing to wait on you for however long it took, but I can't gamble with Luc. That is not an option. Too many people have put him in jeopardy, I won't add my name to that list."

"Xander, you can't expect me to change just like that." She snapped her fingers. "I love you. I love everything about you, but I can't lose myself in our relationship and you don't want me to set a wedding date based on Luc. That's not fair to either of us."

He spun around. The tortured glare that marked his face was hard to witness, but she loved him too much to dangle hope that she wasn't sure she could deliver.

"I know that. You take the time you need, but I want to do it the old fashion way."

"You want me to move out?" The look in her eyes said he should have taken a knife and carved her heart out. He stood across the room as if she was contagious. The distance was developing already. "It's not that I'm asking you to move out, but I don't want Luc to think you're going to be here for him if it isn't permanent. We need to back things up to dating, because that's what we'll be doing."

"You've given this more thought than I realized."

"I have to."

She reached for her robe and tightened it around her, holding the cloth closed at the nape of her neck. "Okay, the Macklemore house is empty. I'll contact the listing agent to see if I can rent it. I should be out by the end of the day tomorrow, or would you want me to be further away? If this is a break-up, please say so. Let's not pretend anything else."

In two strides, he came to his knees beside her. He clasped his fingers around hers. "We're not breaking up. It's not like that." His words tumbled from his mouth. "Tell me you understand."

She'd never lied to him and this didn't seem like the time to start. "I'm not sure I do, but I understand you need to put Luc first."

"I'm not putting him ahead of you." His voice was marked with sharp disappointment.

She touched her index finger to his lips. "Xander, we're not going to second guess each other or place blame. Luc is the only one who matters right now. If you did it any other way, you wouldn't be the man I love. I only have one request."

"Anything."

"Can you sleep in another bedroom tonight? It might make this a little easier if that's possible?"

He lingered on his knees, his anguished face staring up at her. But there was nothing she could do to ease the unhappiness either of them felt. If she had some magic words or a fairytale wand, she'd wave it around and erase her doubts, ease his angst, and set the world back on the right course.

He jumped up. "I need to take a swim."

"It's late. Can it wait till morning?"

"I can't. I just can't." He charged out of the room. She knew he was as close to tears as he could get.

CHAPTER 45

X ander snatched open the front door and charged down the hill. It was well after midnight. No one would be out to notice he was wearing briefs. The only thing that mattered was putting some distance between him and Olivia, a feeling that was as foreign as being a full-time father. He'd made the right decision for Luc, that's what a good parent should have done. Too bad neither Kais nor Eliza had put his welfare above their own.

It would have been nice to have a light breeze to cool his already scorched emotions, but this time of year the humidity stuck around day and night. The cloudy sky made everything darker than normal. Even the water, which was normally turquoise, had taken on an inky blue cast. Under any other circumstance, this would have been a romantic evening. But instead of curling up between Olivia's legs, they were moving apart. Even though they hadn't used the word separation, that's exactly what it was. Gradually, they'd drift apart, burdened by the weight of his work, his son, his responsibilities. Maybe he was meant to live his life alone, but at least now he'd have Luc.

At the shoreline, he listened to the waves lap against the shore. The soothing sound didn't work any magic on his nerves tonight. At least the water reaching his toes was cool. He waded into the surf until the water reached his chest. With a short bounce, he pushed off his toes and began to swim. His arms sliced through the waves. The motion freed him from the bonds of responsibility. The exertion was painful on his wounded arm, but he pushed harder.

When his body cried for relief, he turned back toward the shore. This swim was supposed to clear his thoughts and ease the ache. Instead, it had pulled the worries forward, making them bigger and darker. He neared the shore, hoping his body was numb enough for sleep the moment he settled into the spare bedroom next to Luc.

Something or someone was moving. His peripheral vision picked up two figures from opposite ends of the beach moving toward him. A dreadful premonition descended on him. In the darkened water, they hadn't picked him up yet. He calculated the distance from each of them and the quarter mile required to make it up the hill to his house. A vision of Olivia and Luc ran across his mind. He had no choice but to try to get home. He hadn't even locked the door in his haste to get away. He tore out of the water and sprinted across the sand. His tired legs screamed for mercy as he kicked up sand. The moment his feet struck the paved road, he moved fast. He was going to make it. He had to. His family needed him, and he needed them.

The first bullet whizzed by him, making him duck and run in a zig-zag pattern. If he stayed low and close to the edge of the road, he could make it home. The conversation with Olivia had knocked him off guard. He was getting lazy. In the middle of a case, he never let his guard down. But he'd also never loved anyone as much as he loved Olivia. What had he expected from her? She wasn't the kind of women to acquiesce to his demands.

They were getting close. The second bullet tore through his calf muscle and sent him stumbling off the road. He managed to stay upright and continued toward the house. The third bullet pierced his shoulder. Just beyond the road, he dropped to his knee, before falling onto his face. He wanted to crawl the rest of the way, but it was too late.

CHAPTER 46

Any thoughts Olivia had about coasting through the relationship on a cosmic cloud of love that could endure ups and down had burst. For some people, love was easy to find. But she wasn't one of those people. Everything in life for her had been one hard fight. Even the right to live in New York had required a battle with her father and brothers until she proved she was tough enough to move away from home.

She flopped on the bed with her hand above her head. It was useless to fight the pain, so she inhaled and drew in the sadness and melancholy and despair like they were old friends welcoming her home.

The apartment in New York still belonged to her. At least she had the good sense not to sell it. Maybe somewhere inside, she always knew Xander was too good to be true. That the wonderful relationship they had couldn't last forever. Nothing lasted forever.

It was already tomorrow. But thoughts of packing her things were as heavy as Xander's words. She couldn't move down the hill to the Macklemore house and face the chance of seeing him and Luc every day. Pretending they were dating, hoping he'd call, craving his touch.

If she was leaving, it had to be far away. A clean break, none of that lingering around hoping he'd change or wait for her. How pathetic.

She sprang off the bed and made her way to the closet. Her large suitcase was crammed in a corner under a box of winter clothes she'd never bothered to unpack. She wrestled it out from under the clutter and dragged it to the bed. She opened every drawer in the room that contained her things and began throwing items on the bed. The effort kept the pit at bay. There was no time to wonder what if she'd said yes to marrying him right here and right now. She'd do that at another time.

She jerked her head up at the popping sound outside, frozen in place with a handful of panties in mid-air over the suitcase. Gunfire. That was gunfire. And it was just outside. Her heart thundered in her chest as panic rode up her spine. "My god, what is happening?"

She reached for her phone and dialed Jimmie. "Someone is shooting outside the house." She barked into the phone.

"Where is Xander?"

"He's out there. I don't know what's going on or what to do."

"Damnit! When will this stop? I'll be right there. Give me ten minutes."

"Xander might not have ten minutes. Hurry."

"I'm out the door, Olivia." The line went dead.

For the first time in weeks, she knew which was scarier. Living without Xander would make her life an empty shell. Nobody could love her or make her feel as whole as he did. If she had to make a choice, she'd choose his love and the unending suspense that came with it over the safe predictable unloved life she'd have without him.

If someone was trying to hurt him or Luc, she'd walk through every level of Dante's Inferno to save them. She ran to the nightstand and pulled the drawer open. How could she be a mother with a gun in such easy reach for a child? Xander was right, he needed to look out for Luc. She certainly didn't know how. With the Glock positioned in her hand next to her thigh, she started for the front of the house. There it was again, another pop, and now there were voices. Angry voices.

She eased the door open and crouched on the porch. Peering through the railing, she saw a man pummel someone on the ground.

"Where are the paintings?" His tone was savage as he threw another punch.

She had to fight back the sour taste in her mouth. Xander was on the ground. Even though she couldn't see his face, her heart told her. She steadied the gun in her hand and pulled the trigger. She struck the first man in the center of his chest and he fell to the ground. Before the second man could detect her from the squatted position, she fired another shot. The bullet struck his arm and he dropped his gun. Her second shot caught him in the chest.

With both men down, she charged off the porch. Xander didn't move. She dropped to her knees and pulled Xander into her lap. "Xander, are you alright? Please tell me you're okay." She stroked his forehead and left a dark smudge along the hairline. Blood. His blood.

CHAPTER 47

Olivia paced the same strip in the carpet that she'd paced a moment ago and the moment before that and the moment before that. No matter how many minutes ticked off the clock, nothing happened. She spun around and faced Danny.

"Danny, you're sure Luc is okay?"

"Olivia, you asked the same question ten minutes ago. He's with the neighbor. I've called three times so far tonight and he's asleep."

Even though she was being a pain in the ass, there was no disdain in his voice.

"How long has it been? How long has Xander been in surgery?"

Danny waved her over and patted the chair next to him. "Olivia, please come sit down. No matter how many times you walk back and forth, it's not going to speed up the doctors." He patted the chair next to him.

"There was so much blood. So much blood."

"I know." He patted the seat again.

She stared at it, but adrenaline rushed through her veins.

Sitting wasn't going to help. She tightened her arms around her waist. If Xander walked out of her life, she'd be sad, but she could learn to accept his decision. That way there was always hope they'd find their way back to each other. But if he died, then their story was over. Her heart sagged.

She turned around and headed in the opposite direction.

"Jaysa finally got a phone number and address for Lawrence Cistos." Danny leaned forward.

"You think he was behind what happened to Xander?"

"You said they were looking for the painting. If Lawrence had the painting, he'd be satisfied," Danny paused. "I reached out to Mike in New York. He's going to contact Cistos and put him on to the Marcos Cartel. From there, the two of them should fight it out."

"Then they'll leave us alone?" Olivia said over her shoulder.

"I think so." Danny left his chair and came to stand beside her. He wrapped an arm around her shoulder. The gesture gave her little comfort.

"I should have married him the moment he asked me. You know that?" She sniffed back tears. "I love him more than anything. He'd do anything for me and always has. How could I have been so prideful to hold Xander off? He was willing to wait for me however long it took, but Luc changed things." She placed her head against Danny's chest. "Oh my, Danny. What am I going to do? I'd live in any world if Xander is by my side. I want him and I want Luc, and I'll take them any way I can."

Danny patted her back. "You'll get the chance to say all of that. Xander is too tough to die. Keep the faith, Olivia. We've got to believe Xander is going to be okay. And he is, until the doctors tell us otherwise."

CHAPTER 48

X ander wanted to shift his weight to the other side, but every part of his body ached. The parts of him that weren't covered in bandages were covered in bruises. Three days of lying in the hospital on his ass only made him more grumpy. He glanced at Omar who was seated in a wheelchair near the foot of the bed. He'd been staring at his phone for the last fifteen minutes.

"Are you here to visit me or are you going to make love to that fucking phone?"

Omar dropped the device in the lap of his hospital gown. "Well, you must be feeling better. Back to your mean self."

"I feel like shit."

"You ought to be happy you can feel anything. You almost didn't make it, buddy. The two of us came pretty close to meeting our maker. And neither of us has repented enough for that yet."

Xander looked away from his assistant. "Of course, I had to make it. I'm a father and Luc needs me."

"What about Olivia?"

Xander held up his hand. "Olivia is staying with Luc until I get out of the hospital. After that…"

"What happens after that, Xander?"

"Can you shut the fuck up? Let's talk about something else. Are we all finished with that Cistos business?"

"According to Mike, that's all done. I think the Marcos cartel—the few idiots that are awaiting trial decided to give Cistos his property. Of course, that was only after a few of them ended up in the East River."

"East River?"

"Just a figure of speech, but they're just as dead."

"Any word on Eliza?"

"None. You might as well get used to that."

There was a light rap on the door. Xander glanced at Omar.

"Don't look at me, I'm not expecting anyone." Omar picked up his phone.

The door pushed open and Olivia walked in holding Luc's hand. If goddesses walked the earth, then they looked like Olivia. Her curls were loose and shining liked polished gold. Her bronze skin glowed and she wore a gown befitting a queen. The bold yellow, green, and blue African print matched the tie around Luc's neck.

"What?" He pushed up in the bed.

Luc stood beside Omar's wheelchair and Olivia made it to his bedside, gliding across the tiled floor like an angel. The smile on her face was as welcoming as her body language. After the way he broke off their relationship, he expected harsh words and daggers.

She bent low and pushed aside the material of her bodice. He leaned forward. Her cologne was heaven sent. Just above her left breast his name was scripted on her skin. Her tattooed skin was still puckered and angry.

"You did that for me?" he croaked.

243

"For us."

"What's going on, Olivia? You look gor—gorgeous." Xander tried to find better words to describe her appearance, but his mind had stopped functioning.

"Two years ago, you asked me to marry you." She spoke low, but her eyes were bright. "Do you still want me to be your wife?"

He reached for her hand, ignoring the pain that zipped through his shoulder. Nothing could stop him from touching her. "Of course, I do." The words stumbled out of his mouth. "But is that what you want? Or are you feeling pressured?"

"What I'm feeling is love." She brushed away a tear. "Will you marry me, right here, right now?"

He looked to Omar and Luc. Each of them wore a stupid smile. "You knew about this, Omar?"

His assistant shrugged. "Maybe I did, maybe I didn't."

Xander turned his attention back to Olivia. "You're serious?"

"I've never been more serious. I want to spend the rest of my life next to you and Luc. Nothing else matters."

"Yes, of course, I will. You're the only person I've ever wanted to be my wife—to spend the rest of my life with."

Olivia nodded to Luc and he walked to the door and opened it.

"What's going on, Olivia?"

She held out her hand to Luc who ran to her side. "We're getting ready to have a wedding," Luc said.

Miles walked into the room, followed by several others. "Hirono is here as the minister to perform the ceremony. Miles is going to take pictures. Omar is your best man, and Luc is going to be my son of honor. Later, we'll do the big ceremony with our families, but the most important people are here now." She beamed at Luc.

Xander closed his eyes. His heart was slow to absorb

what was happening. When he opened his eyes, nothing had changed. Everyone was assembled around the bed and the way Olivia beamed said her heart was with his.

"You've made me the happiest man on the island. What can I say?" Xander asked.

Olivia bent over and pressed her lips to his. "Say I do."

ABOUT THE AUTHOR

Jacki Kelly has written dozens of short stories and several books. She lives in the North East with her husband and one loveable dog. She loves hearing from her readers so please contact her.

Connect with her online:
http://www.jackikelly.com

If you enjoyed reading Trouble In Paradise, please tell everyone you know. Please post a review for other readers on your favorite reading forum.